# HIDDEN

## The Gilbert Girls, Book Four
### by Cat Cahill

# Chapter One

C rest Stone, Colorado Territory, 1875
      Dora Reynolds despised ironing tablecloths. Yet she volunteered for the task as often as possible, and then usually pressed a good number of bed linens too, even though those were the maids' responsibility. Being indispensable ensured she kept her position as a Gilbert Girl at the Crest Stone Hotel and Restaurant. Dora was no stranger to hard work, but sometimes she wondered why she'd chosen such a despicable chore. Surely she could have been just as useful collecting the dirty pitchers and glasses at the end of the meal service, as Millie often chose to do. Or delivering Mrs. McFarland, the hotel's bookkeeper, her evening coffee and dessert as Edie often did.

"Miss Dora, you don't need to do that. I've been sent to iron the bed linens." A wispy young girl clung to the doorframe. She was so small, Dora thought she might blow away if she let go.

Dora tucked a piece of her dark hair behind her ear before setting the cooling iron on the small stove. "It's no worry, Helen. I've already finished."

"Thank you, then. You're such a help to us. I'll be sure to let Mrs. Wilson know."

"Please don't. I have no need for accolades. I only want to help." Dora folded the linen on the board and prayed Helen wouldn't say a thing to Mrs. Wilson. The head housekeeper might tell Mrs. Ruby, the dining-room manager. There was a fine line between being necessary and standing out, and Dora couldn't afford the latter.

Helen twisted her hands uncertainly. "All right. You have my gratitude, though. And that of the other girls."

"That's all I need," Dora said with a smile. She placed the folded bedsheet on top of the others before leaving.

The hallway that led back toward the lobby was empty. It was late, and most of the hotel's guests were either in their rooms, or in the parlors on the other side of the hotel. Dora walked silently past the hotel offices, closed for the night, and guest rooms before emerging in the lobby. A handful of guests sat around the fire that still roared in one of the large stone fireplaces. She was just about to move toward the nearby staircase when voices from the lobby desk made her pause.

"Are you certain?" Mr. McFarland, the hotel's manager, asked, his Irish brogue more serious than Dora had ever heard it.

"I am. I've gone over the past week at least five times. The income on the books is not what we have in the safe," Mrs. McFarland said.

They were silent, and Dora flattened a hand on the wall, her heart pounding in her ears. She should not be eavesdropping, but her legs wouldn't move. The worst part about working so hard to be unnoticeable was that on occasion, she heard things she ought not to have heard.

"Please go over the books yourself. If I look at them again, I'll scream." Mrs. McFarland's strained voice sounded on the verge of tears. "What will Mr. Gilbert think if we can't make the sums add up?"

There was another pause, and Dora thought for certain the entire lobby could hear the blood rushing through her ears.

"I'll look at it tonight." Mr. McFarland's voice was muffled, and Dora could imagine him pressing his face to his wife's head, comforting her.

What would it be like to have someone who cared for you so deeply, the way the McFarlands did for each other? Just the thought made Dora's heart ache. She had a mother, cousins, and all sorts of family, but they weren't here. She knew she should count herself luckier than some of the girls at the hotel. Her family was in the Territory, two or three days' ride from Crest Stone, and not hundreds of miles across the country.

Of course, she couldn't tell anyone that. As far as everyone at the hotel knew, Dora Reynolds came from Chicago. And it needed to remain so.

While thinking of her family made Dora long for the comfort of their presence, there was something else that pulled at her heart. Something she'd felt only at her childhood friend's marriage ceremony, at her oldest cousin's smile when speaking of his intended, at—

"There you are!" Penny, one of the girls Dora had arrived in Crest Stone with the previous spring—and now one of her closest friends—emerged from the stairs. "I thought you might be pressing the cushions on the chairs by now. What's kept you?"

"I . . ." Dora couldn't put the words together. She'd overheard something she knew she shouldn't have, so she couldn't speak of the McFarlands' conversation. And now she'd been dreaming away her loneliness in the hallway, and that wasn't anything she wanted to share either, though Penny would be quick to comfort her.

Penny smiled. "It doesn't matter. Come." She grabbed hold of Dora's hand and pulled her up the stairs. "I'm torn between a wedding indoors and one out in the courtyard. Millie and Adelaide insist it's far too cold to stand outside, but I think the snow would be just lovely. Can you imagine? I'd have to write and tell all those old biddies back in Wilmington that I was married in the snow. They'd never believe me. What do you think?"

Dora tried to focus on Penny's locomotive-quick words, and not on the strange tug on her heart or the words she overheard downstairs. "If the ceremony isn't too long, I don't see why you couldn't hold it outdoors."

They arrived at the top of the stairs and Penny nearly whooped with joy. "I knew you'd understand! Outside it is. Oh, I do hope snow is falling that day." Her eyes shone, and while Dora couldn't be happier for her friend, Penny's elation made her even more aware of the pang in her heart.

She was foolish, wishing for such things. Despite Penny's happiness, she no longer had a position within the Gilbert Company. She was allowed to remain at the hotel until her wedding because the McFarlands were generous and kind, but she no longer earned money to send home. Gilbert Girls were not allowed to be courted, and losing her position was not a risk Dora was willing to take. Her family needed her wages. And who would court her anyway, when she could tell him nothing of her past, her family, her home?

After all, the Gilbert Company employed only white women of good standing. Such as Eudora Reynolds of Chicago. But Dora, a girl of the Muache band from the Ute reservation who used her long-absent white father's name, had no place here.

# Chapter Two

Denver, Colorado Territory

Errand boy.

That's all he was to them. Jacob Gilbert grimaced as he slid the soles of his shoes against the boot scraper near the front door of his family's company office. His father and older brother were far too busy conducting business to be bothered to walk to the postmaster's or the telegraph office, especially in the wet cold of late November. Those menial jobs fell to the wayward younger son. The one whose shoes were now covered in mud and horse dung from crossing the streets.

He supposed this was why his brother had taken to wearing boots. This territory was still something of a foreign beast to Jacob, and as much as it pained him to admit James knew better, he recognized his brother likely did in this instance.

"Your father's asking for you." T. Pendleton Clark—a long name for a short man—emerged from inside. He served as the Gilbert Company's clerk, and, Jacob had noticed, had the uncanny ability to appear when one least expected him.

"Did he give a reason?" Jacob gave up on his ruined shoes and moved to the door.

Clark shook his head. "No, sir. But he was insistent I find you immediately."

Jacob deliberated as he turned the knob. Perhaps this was the opportunity for which he'd been waiting these few weeks, a chance to prove he was ready to take on a larger role within the company, an opportunity to do something other than deliver mail or escort visitors from the depot.

Or it could be that his father needed a hot meal, and Jacob was just the person to fetch it.

He shrugged off his coat and gloves, and hung those with his hat before striding down the hallway toward his father's office in the rear of the building. He peered into James's office on the way. Empty. So this would be a meeting among the three of them. That could bode well . . .

Outside the door, Jacob took a moment to straighten his vest and jacket before knocking.

"Where have you been?" his father barked as James opened the door.

"I sent that telegram—"

"Sit. I have an appointment at three, and this matter has already taken too much of my time." Father waved at the red-cushioned chairs opposite his desk, against which he stood. James Gilbert, Senior cut an imposing figure, not only in dress but in manner. Jacob assumed that half the time his father got his way simply by intimidating people with his mere presence.

Jacob glanced at his brother as they sat, but James Junior raised his considerable eyebrows, a younger replica of their father's, as if to say he didn't know what was to come. James's glance traveled to Jacob's mud-encrusted shoes. Jacob resolved to purchase boots on his way home this evening.

"I'll make this brief. We have an embezzler at one of our hotels. I've sent Clark out to the telegraph office to notify the Pinkerton Agency that we're in need of their services. I imagine they'll send a man out immediately. James, I'll need you to deal with him. Jacob can ensure he has all he needs to make the journey south." Father paced the room, speaking as quickly as possible. Jacob had the distinct impression his father regarded this entire matter as a disruption to his usually well-scheduled day.

"I'll take care of it," James said. "Which hotel?"

"The new one south of Cañon City. Crest Stone."

James nodded. "Dare I ask how much was taken?"

"Too much. It appears to have happened over the course of a week or so. The manager can't make sense of it. If it continues, it could endanger the financial stability of the hotel. I haven't closed an establishment yet, and I don't intend to start. Make sure the Pinkerton knows that." Father's face grew red as he spoke. It was as if the thief had come to Denver and plucked the money straight from his pocket. Whoever found the embezzler and put an end to his crimes would receive the eternal gratitude of the Gilbert Company. Perhaps . . .

James asked another question, but Jacob didn't hear it. An idea began forming, grew as his father answered, and demanded to be heard.

"We don't need the Pinkertons," he blurted out.

Father stared at him, struck without words for possibly the first time in his life. "And what do you propose instead, Jacob?"

"Me."

"You're joining the Pinkertons?" James sat up in his chair.

Jacob stood. He had to phrase this perfectly, or Father would never agree. "I propose to send myself to the Crest Stone Hotel to fulfill some necessary position. Assistant to the manager, perhaps. I'll take an assumed name, conduct an investigation, and uncover the thief." He forced himself to remain still, every inch the assured businessman, just like his brother.

Father studied him, running a hand over his salt-and-pepper beard. James appeared struck dumb, his mouth open.

Before either could speak, Jacob anticipated their first question. "I may not be experienced in such things, but if I succeed, we'd save needing to pay the Pinkertons. And I have a personal stake in rooting out the thief as quickly as possible. Give me two weeks. If I fail to solve our problem by then, I'll return home and you can send in the Pinkertons." He pressed his lips together and waited for Father to speak.

A slow smile spread across the man's face. "I'll agree, but only because I'm pleased with your initiative for the company, Jacob. You have two weeks. Don't disappoint me." And with that, he was out the door, off to his appointment.

It had worked. Jacob stared at the empty doorway, half expecting his father to return and change his mind.

"That was bold," James said from behind him.

Jacob turned. "I'm not sure I expected him to agree."

"You know he'll send you packing back to New York if you don't succeed, right?"

The truth struck Jacob to the core. His brother was right. Father wasn't one who handed out second chances. "I won't fail."

"I hope you don't." James smiled and thumped Jacob on the back. "Else you'll find yourself assisting our dear sister with her wedding plans."

Jacob groaned. On his last visit home, the eldest of his younger sisters had chattered nonstop about the color of table linens and the cut of her wedding dress. It was more than a man could bear.

"You might also want to purchase some boots before you leave if you have any hope of fitting in." James eyed his brother's ruined shoes.

Jacob laughed. "I believe I will."

"Good." James studied him a moment, his face growing serious. "You've grown up, little brother. I don't know that Father believes that yet, but this is your opportunity to prove it to him."

"I'm aware," Jacob replied. He gave his brother a wry grin. "I left my old ways in Chicago. As many as I possibly could, anyhow." It was a minor miracle that their uncle hadn't booted him out of his small meatpacking business, given Jacob spent more time chasing down entertainment than actually working.

"Prove it to Father, and you'll have a permanent place in the company."

"I intend to." Jacob made his way to the door, then paused. "Thank you."

"Go pack your things. I'll send a telegram to Crest Stone and arrange a position for you there."

As Jacob collected his hat and coat and stepped out into the biting early winter chill, he couldn't keep the grin from his face. He'd prove to his father he was a Gilbert not just in name, but in action. No more gambling or drinking, and certainly no more women. He'd secure a position in the company, and put his wild past to bed for good.

# Chapter Three

Dora slipped silently out of her room. Her roommate Millie had still been asleep and wasn't scheduled to work until the lunch shift, and Dora hated to wake her this early for no reason. Two other girls rounded the corner to the stairs, also on their way to work the breakfast shift. It was early, but Dora didn't mind that. Breakfast was the easiest meal to serve at the hotel because there was no train. Only hotel guests came for breakfast, and they were in no hurry.

She turned the corner and collided into something—or *someone*—tall and broad.

"Oh!" Dora squeaked as hands gripped her arms and held her steady.

The man stepped back. "I apologize. Are you hurt?"

"Only surprised." Dora intended to excuse herself and continue on her way downstairs, but instead, she glanced at the man's face. Eyes as gray as the winter sky stared back at her. He smiled, and it seemed as if her legs no longer worked as legs should.

He shifted his gaze to his hands, which somehow still held her arms. He let her go, not quickly as she'd expected, but slowly, as if he was afraid she'd topple over without his assistance. The smile never left his face.

The man inclined his head slightly and stepped to the side to let her pass. "Take care with these corners," he said, his voice alight with mischief.

Words flew about inside Dora's head, but none seemed to come together into any sensible speech. She bit her lip, just in case the Ute language decided to make itself present instead. Dora spoke perfect English, which was part of the reason she and her mother decided Dora would be the one to find work. The man took a step forward, straight into the women's dormitory hall.

"You aren't allowed there," she finally said.

The man paused. "Pardon?"

"That's the women's dormitory. For female employees of the hotel . . ." She trailed off. Who was this man anyway? If he worked here, she certainly hadn't seen him before. But asking felt much too forward. Simply running into the man had felt too forward, particularly for someone who wished her entire existence at this hotel to be unnoticeable.

"It is?" The man's gaze roamed the hallway, and Dora half expected one of the other girls to step out just at that moment. What would she do then?

"Yes. The men's quarters are in the other wing. I'm sorry, I've presumed you work here . . ." Dora didn't dare phrase that as a question. In fact, her face went warm the second the words were out of her mouth. What must this man think of her? She hoped he wouldn't think of her at all after this incident. Forgettable—that's who she needed to be.

He graced her with that smile again, and it felt as if she'd developed fever. "You presumed correctly. I apologize again—I've forgotten my manners. I'm Jake James, the new desk clerk. And it appears as if you are one of the illustrious Gilbert Girls."

"Miss Reynolds," Dora supplied. She had a million questions. Hadn't Mr. McFarland shown him around? Hadn't he told this Mr. James of the rules? What possessed the man to wander about the women's dormitory wing? Where had he come from? And why, for all good things, could she not look away from those eyes?

She remained silent.

"It's a pleasure to make your acquaintance, Miss Reynolds. May I escort you downstairs?"

Dora pressed her lips together. How was it possible to want something and not want it at the same time? They both needed to go downstairs, though, and she supposed it would be rude to refuse. There was nothing untoward about running into another hotel employee while on her way to the dining room. After all, she'd traversed these stairs many times with other desk clerks, kitchen boys, and other men who lived in the opposite wing. Why should this feel any different?

*It isn't*, she told herself as Mr. James gestured for her to go first. As they descended, it became evident he was much more the conversationalist than she.

"How long have you worked for the Gilbert Company, Miss Reynolds?" he asked at the top of the stairs.

"Since May. I was among the first group of girls to arrive here."

"And how do you find your work?"

"It's fulfilling. This is a good company to work for."

"Do you have many friends here?" They'd reached the middle of the staircase.

"I do." Somehow, despite keeping to herself, she'd found friendships with several of the other girls. After all, they'd all been thrown into this new and uncertain situation together. She supposed it was only natural they'd seek each other out for companionship.

"And where do you call home?"

Dora paused. He was awfully inquisitive. Was this a natural trait, or was there something about her that had aroused his curiosity? "Chicago," she said carefully.

Mr. James's bright smile grew even wider. "Chicago! I spent—pardon me—I hail from that fair city myself."

Dora's heart nearly leapt out of her throat. She should have chosen someplace less populated. She'd already dodged acquaintance with a couple of the other girls who came from Chicago, and now there was Mr. James.

"Tell me, how do you think the frontier compares to such a vibrant city?" he asked.

"I prefer the Colorado Territory." It was an easy answer, considering Dora had never set foot outside the Territory.

"You have a wandering heart, then." Mr. James must have meant that as a compliment, given his smile hadn't diminished one bit.

When they reached the bottom of the stairs, he took her hand, kissed it, and said, "Well, it has been a pleasure to converse with you, Miss Reynolds. Thank you again for saving me from breaking the rules. Now, I must be off to my duties." He left her standing at the bottom of the stairs, feeling as if she'd just survived a whirlwind.

Dora gripped the banister and placed her other hand over her heart. She'd barely spoken more than a few words to the man, and yet she felt as if he knew everything about her. It was a ridiculous notion, of course. There was no reason for him to suspect that she wasn't who she claimed to be.

When her heart finally slowed to a respectable pace, she leaned around the staircase until the front desk came into view. There he was, now conversing with one of the other clerks, a Mr. Graham. Dora only knew Mr. Graham as a pompous sort who came from wealthy family somewhere back East. She would need to cross the lobby—and pass the front desk—in order to reach the dining room. What if Mr. James caught her eye again? Dora didn't know the appropriate response. Should she greet him? Simply incline her head? The whole thing was overwhelming, and it almost made her want to return upstairs and claim to be too ill to work today.

"I can't be late if you haven't arrived yet!" Adelaide Young, the newest Gilbert Girl, came flying down the stairs.

Dora tried to push Mr. James to the back of her mind. She had work to do. "I . . ."

Adelaide tilted her head. "Is everything all right? You seem distracted."

Dora shook her head, hoping the action would clear her mind of Mr. James. "I'm fine. Come, let's get to the dining room, or we will be late!"

Adelaide looped her arm through Dora's. It was such a small gesture, and the other girls did it all the time, and yet Dora always felt strange about it. As if she didn't truly belong here. Or perhaps it was guilt from the lies she'd been forced to tell in order to remain in the hotel's employ. She tried to relax . . . until they passed the front desk.

She couldn't help but look, and just as she did, Mr. James turned that smile toward her again. Dora's face flamed, and she ducked her head.

Adelaide looked between them. "He's a handsome one, and it looks as if he knows it too."

Dora said nothing, and thankfully, Adelaide didn't press the issue. Instead, she chattered the rest of the way to the dining room about how she needed to work on serving her tables faster and how thankful she was that the breakfast service didn't require her to do so.

When they arrived in the dining room, all thoughts about Mr. James flew from Dora's mind when she spotted Mr. McFarland in conversation with Mrs. Ruby. They could have been speaking about anything, but the words she'd overheard a few days ago immediately came to mind. If the McFarlands hadn't found the money missing from the account ledger, that could only mean someone had taken it. And from the dark look on Mr. McFarland's face—and the frown on Mrs. Ruby's—it appeared that might be the case.

It was hard to imagine a thief lodging at the hotel. He had to be long gone by now, though. After all, who would steal from a place and then remain there?

# Chapter Four

Snow swirled as Jacob walked from the hotel to the stable. The icy wind bit at his face, and he was thankful he at least knew how to handle the winter cold, even if he was still trying to figure out the customs and requirements of the Territory. He paused to admire the valley, which lay spread out before him, blanketed in soft white. At the bottom of the hill that sloped down from the hotel, the railroad tracks ran the length of the valley, a cut of black against the snow. The little depot and the handful of buildings on the other side of the tracks sat silent, gray smoke pluming from their chimneys. It wouldn't be long until Christmas. What would celebrating that holiday be like in a place such as this? There were no carolers on the streets, no shopping to be done in busy stores, no bustling about to visit or be visited by relatives.

He shouldn't be here by the time Christmas arrived. Jake intended to find the embezzler in a matter of days and return victorious to Denver. He'd set himself the lofty goal of meeting as many of the hotel's employees as he possibly could by the end of the day. He'd introduced himself to the kitchen help and had been promptly shooed out by the head chef. He'd met his three fellow desk clerks, the bellhops, some of the maids (most of whom had stared at him like rabbits looking at a shotgun), the hotel's maintenance men, and a good number of the Gilbert Girls. The latter had been the most fun to meet, he had to admit, although most of them giggled far too much for his liking. He'd had his fill of girls with nothing but fluff between their ears back in Chicago and New York. But the woman he'd met upstairs . . . she was intriguing.

Miss Reynolds had been quiet, almost suspicious of him. He could have smacked himself for not knowing one of his family company's own basic rules. Mr. McFarland had told him all of it upon Jake's arrival, but he hadn't paid much attention. He hadn't thought he needed to. After all, his family owned the hotel, so what was there he didn't already know? Quite a bit, apparently. No one here, not even Mr. McFarland, knew his true identity. And if Jacob wanted it to remain that way, he needed to take more care with his actions. Or else, observant people like Miss Reynolds might take notice.

He had never seen hair that dark. His was a dark brown, but hers was most certainly black. It was almost as if she were born of the night in this wild place. He could hardly place her in Chicago—she seemed much more suited to the wildness of this valley. Her eyes were just as dark as her hair. She must be of Italian or Greek descent. If he got to know her better, he might ask. But as it was, he'd seemed to scare her off with his questions this morning. When he'd seen her twice more today, she'd skittered away in the opposite direction. He didn't know what to make of that. Women generally responded to his congenial manner and the attention he lavished on them. To have one run away was . . . disconcerting. Perhaps she was shy? Although she hadn't seemed to fear telling him the rules. She was quite beautiful, and that was all the more reason for him to leave her be. He had work to do here, and a distraction like Miss Reynolds would only find him packing his bags for New York.

A horse neighed from the direction of the stables, shaking Jacob from his reverie. He'd been on his way to meet the men who worked in the stables when he'd been distracted by thoughts of the mysterious Miss Reynolds. He made his way through the snow to the door. Inside, a few windows lent feeble light. Jacob kept his coat on and let his eyes adjust before looking around.

No one was in sight, but he followed the sounds of conversation to the rear of the building. Two men shoveled old straw into a cart.

"Good afternoon," Jacob said, removing his hat.

"Afternoon," the taller man said, while the shorter, rounder fellow merely grunted and went back to his work.

"I'm Jake James, newly employed at the hotel."

"Good to meet you, James. I'm Will Adkins, newly employed myself. And that's Frank Robbins. He's been here a spell." The tall man set his shovel aside and held out a hand. Jake took it, thankful at least one of the men was interested in speaking with him.

"How do you find your new work?" Jacob asked.

Adkins shrugged, adjusting his starched, well-pressed shirt. "It's work. I've always been partial to horses, so I'm happy enough. What is your position here?"

"New front desk clerk. Where do the two of you come from?"

"Everywhere," Adkins said with a laugh. "Robbins there . . . well, I don't know where's he from."

Robbins grunted again. Jacob talked a little longer to Adkins about horses, not that Jacob knew much about the beasts himself. They were good for carrying a person from one place to another, and exciting to watch in a race, but that was the extent of his knowledge. Adkins, however, was a veritable horse expert. The man was night and day from his colleague, not only in amiability, but in dress and—Jacob tried not to breathe too deeply—in hygiene. Robbins appeared to have slept with the horses, while Adkins could have easily walked into the Crest Stone Hotel's dining room for dinner.

Jacob left the stables feeling accomplished. He hadn't yet met the blacksmith, the depot clerk, or the general store owner, but considering those individuals didn't make their residence within the hotel, he supposed he could remove them as possible suspects.

The next task he had devised for himself was to seek out the office in which the hotel funds were kept. James had shown him the original blueprints for the building, indicating the safe was located in the manager's office. Jacob only needed an excuse to be in that room to see it firsthand.

He entered the hotel through the kitchen door in the rear, just in time for the employees' supper. Gilbert Girls, maids, handymen, and anyone else who worked at the hotel came and went from the kitchen, eating as their work allowed. Jacob's shift had ended that afternoon, and so he lingered at the table, talking and listening to those around him, hoping to pick up some necessary bit of information. But nothing he overheard or was told struck him as important.

He stirred his soup as an image of his father dismissing him back to Manhattan came to mind. It was imperative that Jacob find the thief. Banishment to the family home in New York ensured he'd be cut from the business. And unless he wished to live with his mother and unmarried sisters for the remainder of his life, he'd need to find another place for himself. While his family name might open doors for him, he'd be starting from the bottom. That would mean years before he earned an income decent enough to persuade a woman to marry him. Years before he could afford a home of his own.

The spoon stilled in his soup, and Jacob could have laughed. Here he was, Jacob Gilbert, life of the party in college in New York and all the most popular establishments in Chicago, worried about being unable to settle down and start a family. He had changed, even if his father couldn't see it.

McFarland entered the kitchen from the dining room and took a seat at the table. The timing was perfect. Jacob finished his soup, returned the dirty dishes, and left through the back door. Re-entering the hotel from the garden door that opened into the north wing's hallway, he found the hotel office only a door down. It was shut.

Glancing around to ensure no one was in sight, Jacob tried the knob, hoping no one was inside. The door was locked. He stood there for a moment, contemplating his options. Was it necessary for him to lay eyes on the safe if he knew where it was? Perhaps he only needed to keep watch around the area for . . . what, exactly? It wasn't as if the thief would stroll right by him and break into the room. No, whoever he was, this embezzler was much more devious.

James had given him all the information he'd learned from McFarland before Jacob had left Denver. The stolen sums had occurred over the course of ten days, and the best they could figure, it had happened approximately three separate times.

The thief clearly knew when the office was unlocked and knew the combination to the safe. Jacob would need to find a way to set up a hidden watch, without anyone being the wiser.

He turned to make his way back to the kitchen, where he figured he might as well sit and attempt to gain more information. The last door in the hallway on the right opened just as he moved past it. He darted quickly out of the way, only to find himself standing directly in front of the one person he'd thought about most that day—the dark-eyed beauty he'd spoken with first thing that morning.

# Chapter Five

A little shriek slipped from Dora's mouth when a man suddenly appeared in front of her. She clutched the freshly pressed tablecloths she held to her chest and willed her heart to slow down.

"We meet again. I apologize for startling you. Again." Mr. James's soft gray eyes traced her face, and Dora thought she'd melt into the floor. Only a heap of perfectly unwrinkled table linens would be left behind.

"You seem to need to apologize fairly often," she said, then clamped her mouth shut. Where had that come from?

He laughed. "Apparently, I do. At least when I'm in your vicinity."

Dora nudged the laundry room door shut with her elbow. "I must get these to the dining room before the start of the dinner service."

"By all means. I'll carry them for you."

"That isn't necessary. This is part of my work."

"Nonsense. What sort of gentleman would I be if I didn't offer to carry a lady's load?"

Dora paused a moment, then let him take the linens. His eagerness reminded her of some of the boys she'd known in winter encampments, before her family had been forced onto the reservation. The thought made the corners of her mouth rise.

"Your smile is quite becoming," Mr. James said.

His words made her go warm from head to toe all over again. She immediately resumed her usual stoicism and tried in vain not to wonder why he'd said such a thing. It wasn't something she was *allowed* to wonder. "Were you going out of doors?" she asked, hoping to avoid the subject of her smile.

"Yes. You'll be pleased to know I was following the rules this time."

Dora raised her eyebrows in question.

"'No walking through the dining room during meal services.'" He imitated Mr. McFarland's brogue.

Dora clutched her lip between her teeth to keep from laughing. "You do know there is a door from the kitchen to the south wing hallway?"

"I did not. And so therefore, I risked freezing to my death by walking through the garden to return to the kitchen," Mr. James said.

Just as they reached the end of the hallway, Millie appeared from the staircase. She passed them, grinning at Dora. Dora sighed inwardly. Millie would want to know everything later that evening.

Mr. James continued talking, as if Millie hadn't even passed by with that knowing look on her face. "Although, as cold as it is out there, it has nothing on the wind whipping off Lake Michigan." He looked at her as if he expected her to agree.

Dora had only heard of Lake Michigan in passing, and if he'd shown her a map, she wouldn't have even the slightest idea where it was located. She'd chosen Chicago on a whim because she liked the way the name sounded, but she knew nothing at all of the city. She presumed Lake Michigan must be near Chicago, and so she nodded in agreement. That seemed to appease him.

"I don't miss the wind at all, I must say. Although my uncle's business—where I worked when I lived there—was located far enough away I didn't need to feel it on a regular basis. Did you live near the lake?"

Dora searched the lobby in a desperate attempt for an escape from this conversation. If she said yes, would he ask her more? He might if she said no, too. What if she accidentally said she lived in a wealthy part of town? *Was* there a wealthy part of town? There were too many opportunities to mess this up. It was best not to answer at all, but how could she do that without seeming rude?

They were passing the small grouping of chairs that sat facing the north stone fireplace in the lobby. Dora moved slightly to the left, just close enough to tap one of the chairs with her foot. She pretended to stumble forward.

Quicker than a mountain lion, Mr. James caught her with his left hand, still balancing the tablecloths with his right. "Are you all right?"

"Yes, I believe so." Only after she'd spoken did Dora realize she was clinging to Mr. James's arm. She quickly drew her hands away and prayed no one had seen. "Thank you for your assistance."

"Of course." Mr. James tilted his head as he studied her. "Are you feeling well? You seemed to have lost your balance."

"I . . ." It was best to agree with him. He must've noticed that she'd veered sideways. "Yes, I feel a bit lightheaded."

"Why don't you sit? I'll deliver these tablecloths and return to see if you're recovered."

"No, I couldn't. We're not—"

"Yes, I know. Employees are not allowed to sit in guest seating. I'm sure this is an exception to that rule, however. I doubt anyone wants you fainting in the middle of the lobby." And with that, he took her hand and guided her to the nearest chair.

His hand was warm despite the chill outdoors. Dora perched on the edge of the seat. When he let go of her fingers, it felt as if she didn't know what to do with her hands anymore. She clasped them together in her lap, trying to recover some of the warmth his grip had given her.

He left to bring the tablecloths to the dining room. Dora glanced around the room, prepared to spring up if anyone were to see her sitting here. But the only people in the lobby were a few guests, most of whom were busy talking or reading, a desk clerk who was deep in conversation with another guest, and one of the newer girls, Edie, who made her way to the front doors of the hotel. The girls working the dinner service would already be in the dining room, preparing for that meal. And she hadn't yet heard the scream of the train whistle, indicating its arrival in Crest Stone and the inevitable influx of guests into the hotel for supper.

She wanted desperately to sink into the luxury of the armchair, but she didn't dare. Finally, Mr. James returned—with Mrs. Ruby in tow. Dora sighed inwardly. The last thing she wanted was special attention from Mrs. Ruby.

The woman leaned down beside her, pressing a hand to Dora's head. "My dear, are you not feeling well?"

"I'm well. I only felt faint for a moment, but it's passed." Dora pushed herself up from the chair, nearly causing Mrs. Ruby to back into Mr. James. "I thank you for your assistance, sir, but I'll be fine now."

Mr. James raised his eyebrows. His face said he didn't believe her. Dora wanted to sigh again. She had become so good at concealing the truth that no one believed her when she spoke it.

"You've been working too hard," Mrs. Ruby said. "I know you like to help, but you ought to have more concern for your own health."

Dora didn't know what to say. She thought she'd been careful not to draw attention to the help she gave the hotel maids, but it seemed Mrs. Ruby knew all about it.

"You're one of my hardest workers. And now I'm telling you to go upstairs and lie down. I'll have one of the other girls take you up."

"I can go on my own," Dora said. "I promise, I'm well."

Mrs. Ruby pursed her lips. After a few seconds, she relented. "All right. I do thank you for being so willing to help around the hotel, particularly since we aren't in a position to hire any additional help at the moment. I only want to ensure you get enough rest, plenty of food, and that you aren't working too hard."

"I'll rest, I promise," Dora said, but it was Mrs. Ruby's other words that lingered in her mind. The hotel wasn't in a position to hire any additional help. That had to be because of the missing money. After all, they certainly weren't lacking guests or customers in the restaurant.

Behind Mrs. Ruby, Mr. James's usual smile had disappeared as Mrs. Ruby spoke. He was new, but he was hired to replace a previous desk clerk. He had to know his position was not in danger.

The train whistle sounded just then, announcing the arrival of many hungry customers.

"I must return to the dining room. I'll see you in the morning." Mrs. Ruby nodded at Mr. James before bustling away.

Mr. James watched her retreat, and then turned back to Dora. "Are you certain you'll be all right on your own?"

His concern was touching, but considering she'd made the entire thing up, it also made Dora want to scream in frustration. "I am. Thank you for your kindness."

"In that case, I'll bid you good evening. I have some important work I must attend to." And with that, he was gone, leaving her wishing he'd felt the need to kiss her hand again.

Dora rubbed her hands against her cheeks, trying to rid them of the odd thought. Mr. James was simply a polite, well-bred man. It was nothing more than that, and she'd be a fool to think otherwise. And if it *were* something more

. . . that would be impossible. Gilbert Girls were forbidden from being courted during the term of their contracts with the company. And then there was
the not-so-small matter of her own background. If he knew she wasn't who she
claimed to be . . .

Dora strode to the stairs. She didn't want to imagine his reaction if he
found out she was Ute. Her white father's looks were the only reason she'd been
able to pretend otherwise, which she did only to obtain this position. She was
not ashamed of where she came from, of her own people. It was quite the opposite. Some nights, she lay awake, dreaming of returning home, even though
home was now the reservation. She missed her mother's flatbread and fruit
cakes, roasting piñon nuts with her cousins, and the easy friendships she had
with the other girls. She'd made wonderful friends here in Crest Stone, but not
a single one of them *really* knew her. Mostly, she missed being herself.

If Mr. James knew any of that, she doubted he would be so kind to her. No
matter how he acted around her now, it was best to keep him at a distance, the
way she did with everyone else here.

It was the only way to keep her position—and her heart—safe.

# Chapter Six

The wind blew Jacob into the small depot down the hill from the hotel. Inside, the little woodstove struggled to heat the waiting room and ticket office. With no more trains or passengers expected for the evening, the building was empty save for the depot clerk.

"Good evening," Jacob called through the ticket window.

The older man ambled over from a seat at a small table. "I was just about to shut the place up. Do you need a ticket?"

"No, sir. I was hoping to send a telegram."

"Well, this is the place." The clerk passed a stubby pencil and a piece of paper through the window.

Jacob scrawled a quick note to his father. *My work here progresses. Have made many friends. Will keep you apprised.* It was just cryptic enough not to raise questions from the clerk, who apparently also doubled as the telegraph operator. He slid the note and pencil back through the window. "It needs to go to Mr. James Gilbert, Sr. of Denver. No relation to the company," he added quickly upon seeing the recognition on the clerk's face. "My mother's people are Gilberts, originally from down South."

The clerk nodded, and Jacob let out a breath. While the older man sent the telegram, Jacob busied himself with warming his hands by the woodstove. The telegraph machine clicked away. Minutes passed, plenty of time in which to send a telegram. Suspecting the clerk thought he wanted to wait for a response, Jacob finally drew himself away from the heat to inform him otherwise. He lowered his head to see through the ticket window, and then nearly hit it against the wooden frame when he saw a woman standing next to the telegraph machine.

"Miss Reynolds?" he called.

She looked up, her pretty face moving quickly from a pleasant smile to alarm. He hoped that was only because he'd startled her, and not because she was anxious to be in his presence again.

"Mr. James," she said.

Jacob winced inwardly at the false name. It had seemed the obvious choice when his brother had sent word to McFarland that a Jake James would be taking the place of their recently departed desk clerk. It wasn't difficult to remember, and it would serve to remind him of everything he stood to lose—all to his brother—should he not succeed. But now . . . he wished to hear Miss Reynolds call him by his real name.

Jacob tried to focus again on the lovely Miss Reynolds. She wore a heavy coat over her dress, the hood thrown back to reveal shining dark hair piled on top of her head. Her broad features wavered between a smile and a look that spoke of a desire to dart out of the depot as quickly as possible.

"I thought Mrs. Ruby told you to rest this evening," he teased, hoping to lighten her mood.

"She did. I . . ." She fingered a small envelope clutched in her hand. "I need to mail my earnings home to my family."

So the depot clerk also served as the postmaster. Jacob hoped the Colorado & New Mexico Railway Company compensated the man well, for all the jobs he appeared to balance. "That is noble of you to do," he said to Miss Reynolds, despite the immediate curiosity that took hold of him. Miss Reynolds' family was clearly in some sort of financial need. Although he should have expected it—after all, one of the reasons the company hired young women was to enable them to support their families if needed. Not many women without such a need would take on work, and especially not so far from home in a place that still retained many of its wild qualities.

"I don't know that it's noble so much as it's necessary," she replied. She handed the envelope to the clerk.

"I'll see that it goes out on the noon train tomorrow," he said.

"I'm grateful." Miss Reynolds drew her hood back up over her hair.

Jacob made his way around the ticket window and through the low door that separated the minuscule office from the rest of the waiting room. The depot clerk looked on the verge of telling him to remove himself back to the waiting room, but Jacob spoke first. "I doubt there will be a response to my message," he said to the clerk. "But if there is, please bring it to me." He fished out some coins from his pocket to pay the man.

The clerk nodded, taking the payment, apparently appeased at Jacob's intrusion into his office. "Your name, sir?"

"Jake James." He held out an arm to Miss Reynolds. "Please, let me escort you back to the hotel, Miss Reynolds."

She hesitated before nodding, but didn't take his proffered arm. "Thank you again, Mr. Thomason," she said to the clerk.

Jacob pushed the back door open. The wind immediately swept in, removing all memory of the heat from the woodstove. Jacob shut the door tight behind him before catching up to Miss Reynolds, who'd already begun the walk up the hill toward the hotel in the dark.

"I don't need an escort," she said, slightly out of breath. "I've walked myself up and down this hill any number of times before your arrival."

Jacob couldn't help the smile that inched across his face. "It would have been rude of me not to offer."

"And that's the only reason you offered?" The second the words were out of her mouth, her cheeks grew ruddy and she looked away.

"You don't often speak your mind, do you?" he asked. "You should. It makes you far more interesting than other girls."

She stopped, the wind lifting the hair that had fallen from its pins and framed her face. "Perhaps we don't care for men to know our true thoughts. Perhaps a woman likes to keep her opinions to herself rather than be seen as unladylike or ungrateful."

"I'm sorry. I misspoke. I only meant to say that I enjoy hearing your opinions."

She crossed her arms, whether against the cold or against him, Jacob didn't know. "You are much too forward," she said.

"I've heard that before," he said with a grin that usually disarmed the girls he met and caused them to laugh.

Miss Reynolds simply stood there, her large dark eyes narrowed, arms firmly wrapped across herself. "However, you also don't speak your true thoughts."

Jacob wrinkled his brow as he shoved his gloved hands into the pockets of his coat. "I'm sorry? I don't quite understand."

She kept that gaze on him, and Jacob was the one disarmed this time. "I read your telegram," she said.

# Chapter Seven

His smile disappeared, and his eyes darted across her face. Dora had needed to gather up every shred of courage she had to confront him with what she'd seen.

"My family wished to be kept apprised of my work here," he said. But he didn't quite meet her eyes.

She kept her gaze trained on him, fighting every urge to accept his answer and quietly look away. Someone had been stealing from the hotel, and she'd be remiss as an employee to ignore suspicious activities such as those of Mr. James. "Surely your work as a desk clerk is not so complicated as to need a report home. Besides, that telegram was addressed to a Mr. James Gilbert, Sr., the owner of the hotel. Not to anyone with your family name, and not to anyone in Chicago."

He said nothing, and she pushed on. "And if you remember, I caught you skulking about the hallway near the offices, when you weren't working. I'd like to know the real reason you're here, Mr. James. And if you don't tell me, I'll be required to alert Mr. McFarland to your . . . activities."

Mr. James rubbed his gloved hands together, glancing this way and that, as if anyone else would be so insensible as to be walking outside in this weather. "Very well. I could use an ally here, and you, Miss Reynolds, are uniquely situated to be just that."

She said nothing, instead waiting for his explanation.

"Let's at least retreat to cover, else we'll freeze in this cold. The smokehouse should serve this purpose well." He started toward the hotel, but Dora remained fixed in place. He stopped and turned.

"I can't be alone with you indoors," she said. Another rule he should know, if he took his job seriously.

"Right," he said. "I'd forgotten."

Dora could have laughed. How ever had he been hired here? He must've charmed his way into this job, since the company prided itself on employing the most upstanding of persons. *Much like you did*, Dora said to herself. Although she didn't suppose it was charm that had landed her a position as a Gilbert Girl—it was sheer determination layered upon falsehoods.

"We'll go to the side of the hotel, then. The north-facing side, where no one can see us. The trees there should break some of this wind."

Dora nodded and followed him as he led the way. As they trudged through the snow on the ground, all she could think of was how she'd avoided telling Millie anything about Mr. James when she asked. And about her friends' stories of meeting their beaux late at night or in secret. Penny told a story of how her now-fiancé taught her how to shoot, alone behind the smithy shop. Emma, since moved to California but on her way back to Crest Stone with her husband, spoke of meeting him in secret by the creek. And even proper, society-minded Caroline met her now-husband for a late-night picnic at an abandoned cabin. Was that what Dora was doing now? Meeting a beau in secret?

A gust of wind pushed her hood from her head and brought her quickly back to reality. Mr. James certainly wasn't her beau. He teased her and had said flattering things once or twice, but she suspected he did that with many women. She knew better than to trust that sort of man. Her own father had been like that, and where had that left Dora's mother? Beholden to her own family, saddened and alone, and embarrassed for marrying such a man. Dora would not follow the same path. She knew better. This meeting was only to discover the reason for Mr. James's presence in Crest Stone. Talking to him now might lead her to help the hotel—and her own position here.

"Warm enough?" he asked as they stopped under a copse of pines and aspens.

Dora nodded. Her people hadn't survived hundreds of years in this valley and others without knowing how to dress when going out of doors. She glanced around. They were secluded, even though the hotel was mere feet away. Secluded enough no one would see them. A thrill shot through Dora's limbs. She'd been so concerned with getting caught and with finding out more about Mr. James that it hadn't occurred to her this could be dangerous. How much did she really know about this man? He was clearly good at disguising his true purpose here. What else was he hiding? Had he lured her here for some other, nefarious purpose? She took a step back, ready to run.

"Please, don't be alarmed." He held both hands up in a gesture of surrender. "I promise you I'm no danger to you or anyone else. Most anyone else," he added. "I'm a gentleman." His voice sounded a bit desperate around the edges, something Dora would never have guessed he was capable of.

"I have no choice but to take you at your word," she said carefully.

He relaxed, dropping his hands and letting his shoulders sink. "You were correct in surmising the recipient of my telegram."

Dora had no doubt about that. There may be more than one James Gilbert, Sr. in Denver, but no others would be on the receiving end of such a message. The depot clerk had likely accepted whatever Mr. James had told him. After all, his discretion was necessary to his work. Not once had he asked Dora why she sent monthly envelopes to the Ute reservation on the southbound trains.

"May I ask why you're sending telegrams to Mr. Gilbert?" Dora was fairly certain she knew the answer, but she wanted to hear it from him.

Mr. James pulled off his hat—a short top hat, much more formal than what most men in Crest Stone wore—and ran a gloved hand through dark hair. "Mr. Gilbert is my employer. I'm here to find a thief." He let the words linger in the chill, the clouds of his breath dissipating as the words hung there.

It was as Dora had hoped. "Do you mean the person who is stealing funds from the hotel?"

Mr. James replaced his hat, fixing her with a surprised look. "You're aware of the situation?"

"I overheard," she admitted. "I've told no one else. But that knowledge is what made me question your telegram. I'd hoped you were on the side of right and not pursuing some sort of extortion from Mr. Gilbert."

He shot that smile toward her again, warm enough she thought the snow might melt from the ground around her feet. "You were right to question me. I'm grateful the company has employees like you on its side, Miss Reynolds."

She warmed under his praise, ignoring the warnings like signal fires in her brain. It was nice to be appreciated, particularly by a man like Mr. James. "I'm happy to help in any way I can."

He took a step forward. "I'm glad to hear that, because I have a proposal for you."

# Chapter Eight

It would be taking a risk to ask Miss Reynolds for her help, and one he certainly hadn't run by his father or brother. But the truth was, he needed help. The hotel was large with many employees. He couldn't keep an eye on them all at once. Having Miss Reynolds on his side would be a blessing. If she agreed, that was.

"Would you assist me in my investigation? It needn't be much. I only need someone to listen and watch, and let me know if there is anyone or anything suspicious about. You're with the waitresses all the time, and often in the kitchen. If you could keep your ears open in that part of the hotel, it would allow me to do the same in the areas where I'm expected to be. We could both work toward the goal of uncovering the thief without arousing suspicion."

Miss Reynolds kept her hands clasped together, her face serious as she seemed to think through his request. "I'll help you," she finally said.

Relief shot through all his senses. With her aid, he might just be able to accomplish what he'd set out to do. He rushed forward, taking her small, gloved hands in his own. "Please accept my gratitude. If the hotel loses too much money, my— Mr. Gilbert will be forced to close it. Together, we can prevent that from happening."

Miss Reynolds stared down at his hands covering hers. With a start, he pulled them away, mentally berating himself for once again being far too forward with her. Such a gesture would have caused the girls he knew in college to smile and bat their eyelashes at him, but it seemed to discomfort Miss Reynolds so. He still couldn't suss out exactly why. She was on the quieter side, for certain, but she wasn't as shy as he'd originally thought. Perhaps she merely feared for her position here. Or she had a man at home waiting on her. The latter thought set him on edge, a bit of anger swirling through the enormity of the relief he felt at her agreement to help.

"Are you a detective then?" she asked, her soft voice nearly whisked away by the wind buffeting the trees.

"Yes," Jacob said before pausing. He hadn't thought through this, since he hadn't planned on revealing himself to anyone here. "I hire myself out as such when people need me."

Dora twisted her hands together, then asked, "How did you become a detective?"

"Well . . ." Jacob trailed off, quickly forming a story. "Back in Chicago, my father was a policeman. I always enjoyed his stories of catching crooks and foiling robberies. An opportunity opened up while I was working for my uncle, I pursued it, and now here I am." It was as vague an explanation as he could possibly give.

"Your family must be quite proud of you," she said.

*They will be*, he said to himself. "They are," is what he really said.

She glanced toward the hotel. "I must return or my roommate will be wondering what became of me."

"Thank you again for your help," he said, forcing himself not to reach for her hand. The last thing he needed was to startle her again.

She lingered a moment, and as he wondered if she was waiting for just such a goodbye, she turned and left for the rear of the hotel.

Jacob leaned against the trunk of a spindly aspen. Miss Reynolds was a conundrum, and the more he spoke with her, the more curious he became.

He just needed to ensure his curiosity didn't impede his work here. And perhaps it wouldn't, now that Miss Reynolds was also working for him. A smile crossed his face at that thought.

Now if only he could remember his own company's rules.

EARLY THE NEXT MORNING, Jacob carried a mug of steaming hot coffee to the hotel offices. McFarland didn't ask for it, nor did he likely need it, but it served as a good reason for Jacob to be in the office. If he could establish this routine, perhaps he'd learn more about the funds that had gone missing.

He paused at the door. Voices came from inside, indistinct and muffled. Jacob leaned in closer. The hall was empty, but he could easily raise his hand and knock if anyone came around the corner. For now, he listened.

It was a man—McFarland, with that accent—and a woman. The woman sounded distraught, but Jacob could only make out bits and pieces of their words. It wasn't enough. He needed to hear more.

Jacob knocked and without pausing, turned the knob. A startled Mrs. McFarland held a large, leather-bound book to her chest, while her husband glared at Jacob. And the door to the safe in the wall hung wide open.

He shouldn't have barged in, but he'd surmised his action was of the rebuking sort and not the firing sort. It was certainly worth it to see that the conversation he'd been overhearing had everything to do with the hotel's finances. Jacob held out the cup and saucer. "I thought you might enjoy some hot coffee, sir."

McFarland's glare lessened into something more of a frown. "Thank you, Mr. James, but I must ask you to refrain from entering rooms without waiting for an answer first."

"My apologies." He nodded at Mrs. McFarland. "Had I known you were here, I would have brought a second cup."

Mrs. McFarland gave him a weak smile. That confirmed it. More money had gone missing, and it must have happened very recently.

"I'll . . . show myself out." Jacob backed up to the door and slipped out.

The door clicked behind him, and Jacob leaned against it for a moment. The situation had grown more dire. He needed to know how much more money had been stolen. He'd need to telegraph James this afternoon, after giving McFarland the opportunity to wire the office in Denver with the latest bad news.

But for now, he needed to find Miss Reynolds.

The breakfast service hadn't yet begun. He didn't know whether she was scheduled, but one way or another, she'd likely make an appearance in the kitchen for her own breakfast. Jacob staked out a corner of the table, heaping servings of eggs, sausages, bread, jams, and cooked oats set out before him. He ate slowly, making small talk with the others who sat nearby, until—finally—Miss Reynolds appeared.

He caught her eye as she made her way to the table, and her cheeks instantly darkened. Just that small reaction warmed him to his core. So she didn't find him nearly as distasteful as she pretended.

She sat directly across from him with her own plate of bread and jam.

"Don't you care for sausage, Miss Reynolds?" he asked. There were far too many ears around to discuss anything serious.

"I'm not used to such things for breakfast," she replied.

Jacob didn't know what to say to that. Everyone he'd known in Chicago ate plenty of meat. Of course, they could afford to do so. Miss Reynolds' family must not have been so wealthy.

They ate quietly for a while. The breakfast service began in the dining room, quickly clearing out most of the remaining Gilbert Girls from the kitchen. As soon as no one was too close to them, Jacob quietly shared the news of the stolen money.

Miss Reynolds drew in a breath. "It must have happened late yesterday."

"Or at night." That seemed the most likely answer. After all, who would steal money when there was a higher probability of being caught?

Across from him, Miss Reynolds sat with a slice of bread in her hand, but not eating. She looked lost in thought, her dark eyes staring but not really seeing. He wondered what it might be like to have those eyes on him all the time. To have her face light up the second she caught sight of him. It would be much harder earned than anything else he'd ever had in his life. He'd never had to work so hard to get a girl to smile at him. He supposed it almost made sense, considering he was here working harder than he'd imagined to obtain his father's approval.

"What is your given name?" he blurted out.

She narrowed her eyes. He was beginning to believe suspicion was Miss Reynolds' default emotion around him.

"I mean, you know mine. It seems only fair I learn yours too." He threw in a smile at the end.

Her face relaxed some, although her eyes darted to the end of the table where a couple of the bellboys sat eating. "Dora," she said, her voice barely a whisper. "It's short for Eudora, but no one calls me that. It was . . ." Her eyes returned to the remaining bread on her plate. "The name of my father's mother."

"It's a beautiful name," Jacob said. "It suits you."

Miss Reynolds—Dora—shifted in her seat, then replaced the slice of bread she'd been holding back onto her plate. "Thank you," she said without raising her head.

Jacob had the distinct feeling she wasn't used to receiving compliments. He had the strongest urge to change that, so strong he almost needed to bite his tongue. When he finally thought he could speak without comparing her hair to the night or her skin to silk or any other pathetic poeticism, he said, "You may call me Jake."

She stared at her bread for a moment longer. "I can't," she finally said. And with that, she rose and gathered her plate and mug of coffee in one quick motion. She was all the way to the boy washing dishes before Jacob caught up.

"Might I ask why?" Jacob placed his own dishes on the counter next to the dishpan.

She whirled around. "It's far too familiar. You don't listen to the rules at all, do you, Mr. James?"

If words could have made him stumble backward, hers certainly would have with their force. But instead of shirking, he grinned at her. "I daresay I've already proven I don't."

She huffed, her hands on her hips.

Before she could say anything else, he added, "It makes no sense, all of this formality, when we'll be working together to save this hotel."

He'd reached her, he could tell. Her hands slowly fell from her hips, and her face softened. "Save? Is it that bad?"

"If the theft continues, then yes. The hotel will close if it runs too low on funds. The company can't pour all of its money into saving a sinking ship."

She clasped her hands together. "All right then . . . Jake."

Even if Jake was a manufactured name, it sounded as if an angel from heaven had spoken it to him. Nothing had ever sounded so sweet. "All right, Dora."

She gave him a tentative smile, and then immediately straightened and replaced it with her usual impassive, slightly suspicious gaze. "I trust you," she said quietly, just as the door from the dining room opened.

Jacob turned. One of the waitresses, immediately followed by another, had entered carrying slips of paper. The first breakfast orders of the morning. "Your trust is not misplaced," he said to Dora, his voice just loud enough for her to hear him, and no one else. "I must get to my post."

The bitter air stung his face the moment he stepped out the door. It bit through the sleeves of his fine jacket, but Jacob barely noticed he wasn't wearing a coat. That tiny smile Dora had given him. The trust she'd placed in him. That was enough to keep him warm through even a blizzard.

# Chapter Nine

The noon meal service started with a frenzy, as it normally did. Dora flew between her tables, the serving stations, and the kitchen, all in an effort to get the train passengers served in under thirty minutes. The hotel patrons knew to wait until the train had left the station before arriving for their own dinners, if they wanted a leisurely meal.

As she worked, Dora watched the other girls. She'd told Mr. James—it still felt too familiar to call him Jake—that she would, but truth be told, Dora couldn't imagine any of these girls doing anything so awful as stealing from the hotel.

And so her thoughts turned to Mr. James. His striking dark hair, the way his eyes crinkled when he smiled, the easy manner he seemed to exude as if he knew the world was his for the taking. How did he go through life like that? Dora didn't know much about life in the city, but she presumed his father might make a decent wage as a policeman. Not enough to join the ranks of the wealthy, but certainly enough so a family wouldn't need to worry about surviving. Perhaps his manner came with that certainty. In a way, it reminded her of some of the young men she'd grown up with, although much of their fire had diminished upon being confined to the reservation. Yes, she decided, Mr. Jake James was very much like a young Muache Ute, ready to face down a bear or raid another tribe.

"What is that silly grin?" Millie asked when Dora wandered toward one of the serving stations. "You look as if you just woke from the most wonderful dream."

"It's nothing," Dora said, falling back to Earth from the sky. "Only a joke from one of my customers."

Millie leaned out to look at the tables that made up Dora's section. "That dour-faced matron and her sleepy husband?"

Dora followed Millie's gaze. Sure enough, only those two remained at one of her tables. Everyone else had returned to the depot.

"*I* believe you were daydreaming about that handsome man I saw you walking with yesterday. You know, the one you haven't yet told any of us about?" Millie filled a water pitcher but kept her eyes on Dora.

"What man?"

"Oh no, you don't get out of it this time." Millie set the full pitcher down and placed her hands on her hips. "We have a moment before we're flooded with hotel guests. Tell me everything. Please." She fluttered her eyelashes at Dora just as Adelaide and Edie joined them with empty water pitchers.

"I fear we missed something fun," Adelaide said to Edie.

"Dora here was just about to tell me all about the gentleman who carried table linens for her. He is *quite* handsome. I believe I've seen him working the front desk," Millie said.

"Oh! The new desk clerk." Adelaide's eyes lit up. "Dora! You didn't say anything about him when we walked by a few days ago." She swatted Dora lightly with her hand.

Edie said nothing, but her smile told Dora that she, too, was waiting. For what, exactly, Dora didn't know. It wasn't as if the man was her beau. And she couldn't tell them about his investigation.

"It's nothing at all," she finally said, her voice a little wobbly. "He saw me struggling to carry the tablecloths and offered to help." That wasn't the entire truth, but at least it wasn't a lie. If she had to spin another falsehood, Dora thought she might lose her mind.

"I'd hoped it was more than that." Adelaide looked as if someone had told her she could never go home again. Millie raised her eyebrows, disbelieving, while Edie shot Dora a sympathetic smile.

She had to give them something, or they'd never let it go. "He is awfully handsome," she finally said.

That was enough to make Millie grin and Adelaide giggle.

"I don't know about you," Millie said, clutching the water pitcher to herself, "but if a man with a smile like that took an interest in me, I wouldn't let him go. Can you imagine never needing to work again? Never having to worry about money or wanting for anything?" Her eyes took on a dreamy look.

"I doubt desk clerks make that much in wages," Edie said.

Dora didn't much care about Jake's—Mr. James's—wages. But she had to admit that his gray eyes and bright smile made her feel as if she'd never be unhappy again.

"Dora Reynolds, you're blushing!" Adelaide said. The girls giggled while Millie gave Dora's arm a squeeze.

"You must promise to tell us if anything else happens," Millie said.

"Nothing will be happening!" Dora stepped back with her pitcher. "I must return to my customers."

That only made them laugh more, and once she'd stepped away from the station, Dora could see why. She still only had the couple, who she suspected were hotel guests that had come down early for the noon meal. The rest of her section was empty.

Undaunted, Dora marched up to their table and poured minuscule amounts of water into their already-full glasses. Then she smiled at the woman's frown and the man's dozing form and asked for their order.

And she prayed the girls' thoughts on Jake could be kept quiet. Being the subject of a rumor was not the best way to remain unseen at the Crest Stone Hotel.

# Chapter Ten

The depot door slammed shut as Jacob stepped out into the snow. Rays of sunlight reflected on the white powder, turning it into diamonds, and people streamed down the hill from the hotel toward the waiting train. He stepped aside, watching as they chatted and laughed. Normally when he felt down, all it took to lift his spirits was surrounding himself with people who were happy. They'd distract him, and once he was alone again, whatever had turned his mood earlier had never seemed as bad.

He didn't have the option to become distracted now. He had to solve his own problem rather than ignoring it. As the train blew its whistle, Jacob climbed the hill. He was due back inside to finish his work shift in twenty minutes' time. Perhaps he'd be able to come up with a solution before then.

He passed between the hotel and the stables with only a vague idea of where he was headed. A break in the tree line loomed ahead. He'd seen this path before. It was just wide enough for a wagon, and was usually trampled down with bits of mud showing under the snow. A fresh layer of snowflakes overnight had covered the path, but recent footprints led the way through the trees.

Jacob followed them and found himself standing beside a half-frozen creek. A small bit of water still ran down the middle, but each side was a sheet of ice. The footprints led to the right, where a small building—presumably the springhouse—stood. No one else had the lack of sense to go wandering about a half-frozen creek in the cold, so Jacob found himself entirely alone for one of the few times since he'd arrived in Crest Stone. The only sounds were the distant neighing of the horses turned out in the corral, the strangled gurgle of the creek, and a rustling from some small creature nearby. The silence pressed on his ears and wrapped around him, foreign and yet, somehow, comforting.

He'd stood there for several moments before he remembered the telegram in his pocket. Peeling off a glove, he fished it out as the irritation and the sheer need to do *something* returned with a vengeance.

*Results needed immediately. Advise on progress by 9 Dec or will send aid.*

Jacob crumpled the paper, his nails digging into his palm. Father had shortened his deadline. He had until the ninth of December, barely a week away. He needed a plan, one that would work and that he could implement right away.

He stood, watching the water make its way slowly down what was left of the creek. He needed something that would draw the thief out. Something irresistible, the way the water was drawn to continue its flow down the mountains and toward the sea.

Money.

Jacob shoved the telegram back into his pocket and returned the glove to his hand. Hotel employees were paid monthly, at the end of each month, so the payroll was out of the question. But perhaps . . .

He smiled at the creek as the barest outlines of a plan formed in his mind. He'd need help to implement it, and luckily, he had just the right person.

JACOB PACED THE LOBBY of the hotel. Guests lingered by the fireplaces on each end, and raucous laughter sounded from the smoking parlor. Only a year ago, he would've found himself drawn to the people, the drink, the cigars, and the games in that room, but none of that interested Jacob now. His shift had ended an hour ago, and he'd forgone supper in an effort to catch Dora as she left the dining room. It was going on nine o'clock. Surely there couldn't be many more guests remaining.

Minutes ticked by. Each time one of the doors opened, Jacob stopped. When yet another guest or two emerged, he sighed in frustration and took up pacing again. A couple of the Gilbert Girls, who must have been off duty since they wore regular clothing, passed by, caught his eye, and giggled amongst themselves. He recognized one, the redhead who had greeted Dora in the hallway last week. The other was a slight girl with mousy brown hair and spectacles. He gave them a quick smile before returning to his pacing.

Finally, the doors opened to a number of uniformed waitresses streaming out, most in pairs, talking together, a few alone, and none of them Dora. Jacob huffed. Where on earth could the girl be? Perhaps she hadn't worked this service and was up in her room, meaning he'd wasted all this time waiting down here. He needed to speak with her immediately. How in the world could he do that when he wasn't even allowed to step foot in that wing?

"You must be the new desk clerk." A younger girl with flaxen hair and a mischievous smile stopped in front of him. A large stain the color of coffee covered her white apron.

"I am," he said cautiously. This girl had the look of one who found trouble easily, and while trouble was something Jacob might've enjoyed in his past, he'd firmly left it there.

She smiled. "I don't suppose you're waiting on Miss Reynolds?"

Had their meetings been that obvious? Or perhaps Dora had mentioned him to this girl? The thought of her speaking to her friends about him made Jacob smile himself. "I might be."

Mrs. Ruby, whom Jacob remembered as the dining room manager and house mother to the waitresses, appeared in the dining room doorway. Her gaze immediately landed on him, and if a frown could knock a person out, Jacob would've wondered how he was still standing upright.

The girl must have felt Mrs. Ruby's disapproval, as she took a step backward from Jacob. "I'll let her know you're waiting in the employees' parlor."

Jacob nodded his understanding, and the girl scampered off toward the stairs. He waited until all the waitresses—and the eagle-eyed Mrs. Ruby—had gone upstairs before retreating there himself.

The employees' parlor was hardly the ideal place to discuss serious matters. The door remained eternally open for propriety's sake, and Jacob counted seven other people inside when he arrived. Nonetheless, it would have to do.

He sat, then stood, then sat again, and stood when a couple of the bellhops attempted to engage him in conversation. Finally, just as he was about to wear a hole in the wood floor from his constant pacing, Dora arrived. She hesitated in the doorway, smiled at a couple of girls on the settee in the middle of the room, and then caught Jacob's eye.

He stood there, rooted to the spot, seemingly unable to breathe for a half a moment. Dora's hair had been hastily put up, and long straight strands of it drifted down, framing her face. The lamplight made her dark eyes glitter, and the smile she bestowed upon him . . . Jacob was certain God had never made anything more perfect.

She glided toward him, walking on clouds, and sat in a nearby chair. "Mr. James," she murmured.

Jacob stood there dumbly before stepping backward and almost falling into another chair. "Miss Reynolds," he managed to sputter. What had gotten hold of him? He'd never had trouble putting words together before, and certainly not with a woman.

"This is highly improper," she said, her voice barely a wisp.

"It is?" Jacob glanced about the room. The bellhops who had tried to engage him in conversation were now talking with a couple of girls. "Doesn't a parlor exist for the purpose of meeting and talking with others?"

"Yes, but . . ." She glanced around furtively, as if someone would jump out and tell her otherwise. "I can't be the subject of gossip."

"I doubt most people want to be," he said, but that didn't seem to soothe the worry that had flattened her lips into a straight line.

"I *can't* be." She gave him a pleading look. More than anything, he wanted to reach out and take her hand and reassure her such a thing would never happen. But he could do neither one.

What he *could* do was change the topic of conversation. "You spoke to your friends about me."

Her cheeks deepened in color, which was exactly the reaction he was hoping to see. She twisted her hands together and then finally spoke. "Are we here to discuss my friends, or did you have something of importance to share with me?"

As much as he'd love to know what she'd said about him, he was also acutely aware that they didn't have much time. It had to be nearing ten o'clock, when all the Gilbert Girls would be spirited away to their rooms, not to emerge until morning. "I have an idea, and I'm hoping you'll help me."

Dora sat up straighter.

"I suspect the money is going missing from the safe since its disappearance isn't discovered immediately. We'll create a story about funds being delivered from the Gilbert offices, and then I'll wait nearby that night to see who comes to take it." He sat back in his chair, hoping she thought it was a good idea.

"Won't people question how we know such a thing?" Dora asked.

"Not if we phrase it in a way that makes it seem as if it's something we overheard."

"Mr. McFarland will surely hear about it, and wonder how such a rumor got started. Shouldn't we tell him your plan?"

Jacob shook his head. It was imperative no one else—not even McFarland—know he was searching for the thief. Not only might it make McFarland suspect Jacob wasn't who he said he was, he had to assume that anyone in the hotel could be the culprit.

*Anyone but Dora.* He could have laughed at the thought, but it was true. He'd made that assumption when he'd told her a sliver of the truth. But it was a ridiculous thought. Dora was hardly the kind of girl who'd go stealing from the safe of the hotel where she loved working.

"We can tell no one. That's important. Do you understand?" he said.

She swallowed visibly as she stared at her hands clasped in her lap. "All right. I understand."

"I highly doubt Mr. McFarland is the person at fault, but we have to assume that anyone could be the thief."

Dora nodded before tilting her face up to look at him. Her dark brown eyes landed on his, and he couldn't look away from her if he'd wanted to. And he didn't want to. His heart lurched into a faster rhythm.

"I want to be there," she said.

"Be there?" The world had faded around him, along with any kind of rational thought. He wouldn't have remembered his own last name—real or fake—right now if someone had asked.

"When you wait for the thief to come."

He blinked at her, everything slowly coming back into focus. Including the ludicrous idea she'd just suggested. "Absolutely not."

She reeled back a little, as if he'd hit her with his words.

"I'm sorry," he said immediately. "I didn't mean to sound so harsh. But it might be dangerous. We don't know who this person is or why he needs the money. And we don't know what he'll do once cornered. Besides"—Jacob gave her his best flirtatious grin—"it'll be past your curfew."

Just as he said the words, the girls who'd been conversing with the bellhops stopped nearby. "Are you coming, Dora? It's nearly ten o'clock," one of them said.

Dora nodded to her before turning back to Jacob. "There are ways around that." She smiled at him, mischief written all over her face, before standing. "I bid you good night, Mr. James."

He'd barely fumbled into standing himself before she was gone, leaving him to ponder the meaning behind her words. If he wasn't mistaken, Dora was playing the coquette with *him*. He'd had plenty of experience in such a thing, and yet now he questioned it. Was he reading something he wished for into her smile and her words, something that wasn't actually there?

He nodded at the other men as they left the room. Dora had his head so muddled he needed a moment to recover. Even if he took her words at face value, it would still be too dangerous. Besides, he needed his wits about him, and those were in short supply when Dora was nearby. If he were smart, he'd end this partnership altogether and find some girl who didn't make him feel the way Dora did to help him out. The last thing he needed right now was to be distracted.

But he had to admit that Dora was more than a distraction. He'd never once taken a woman seriously. Every girl he'd spent time with before was merely a dalliance. A short bit of fun. A distraction from his work or anything else that had been bothering him. He'd never gotten to know any of them beyond what was on the surface.

What would happen if he took a girl seriously? Got to know her, spent time talking about things that mattered, maybe even fell in love? Perhaps Father would respect him more, see him as a man ready for partnership in the company and a family himself.

Images of him introducing Dora to his family flitted through Jacob's mind. She was a waitress, yes, but Father was fairly broad-minded. He might prefer his son marry a girl from a well-to-do family back in New York, but he'd accept who Jacob chose—within reason.

The clock on the mantel struck ten, jarring Jacob from his reverie. He was getting ahead of himself, going from one flirtatious smile to family introductions. *One thing at a time, Gilbert*, he reminded himself. If he didn't keep his attention on catching this embezzler, he could hang all hope of Father's approval, and without that, he wouldn't be able to support a wife and family, much less himself.

# Chapter Eleven

Dora spent the next morning mentioning the "money" that was due to arrive at the hotel on the noon train to a few select girls, ones she knew to have trouble keeping interesting information to themselves. After the evening meal service, she paid a visit to Penny, who was perhaps a little too excited when Dora asked for the best way to sneak out of her room that night. Dora could hardly believe she'd had to ask such a thing. After all, sneaking out—and potentially being caught—wasn't exactly the best way to remain unseen.

But Dora refused to be left out of the one thing that might put this thievery to rest. She wanted to see the person caught. And more than anything, she wanted reassurance that the hotel would continue to operate as it had. Her family was relying on her.

Of course, she said none of that to Penny, who assumed Dora simply wanted to spend time with Jake. Unfortunately, that wouldn't happen at all, since Jake had forbidden her from joining him. But what Jake didn't know wouldn't hurt him.

At precisely half past eleven, as Millie slept curled into a ball, Dora left the room. She couldn't risk getting dressed, and instead pulled a robe tightly around her night things. She'd gone to bed with her corset on, too. If she was caught, at least she'd be halfway properly dressed. She moved like an apparition down the stairs and then through the hallway toward the hotel office. She'd planned her arrival to occur before Jake's, and it looked as if she was successful. She slid behind the door to the laundry room.

There she waited. The minutes dragged on, but her pounding heart kept sleep at bay. Finally, Jake arrived, and Dora guessed it must be about midnight. She pushed the laundry room door completely closed just as he approached the office door. Leaning against the heavy wood, she tried to slow her breathing.

Dora didn't know where Jake planned to wait for the thief. What if he chose the laundry room?

Minutes passed. As her discovery grew less and less likely, Dora's heart slowed to an almost normal rate. She opened the door just a sliver and peered through the crack into the hallway. Her eyes had grown accustomed to the dark, but she couldn't spot Jake anywhere. He must've found refuge in one of the guest rooms along this hallway. As a desk clerk, taking a key wouldn't be such a difficult feat to accomplish.

Dora kept her position behind the door, her eyes on the hotel office. Time seemed to slow to a halt. How long would it take for the thief to make an appearance? She stifled a yawn.

Just as she thought her entire body had gone numb from standing in one position for so long, a quiet shuffling sounded from the end of the hallway, near the stairs.

Dora straightened immediately. It was impossible to know the time, but it was far too late for anyone respectable to still be awake and far too early for any of the hotel employees to be starting work. She squinted through the crack in the door. A shadowy figure emerged, making its way slowly down the hall. As it grew closer, Dora made out a robe and long, undone hair. Red hair.

She threw a hand over her mouth to stifle a gasp. It was Millie. That was impossible. It couldn't be . . .

Millie paused by the office door, her face searching the hallway—until her eyes spotted the laundry room door. Too late, Dora realized she should have shut the door. She took a step back as Millie pulled it open.

"Dora?" she asked, even though it was clear Dora was standing right in front of her.

"What are you doing here?" Dora asked. She didn't want to think that Millie was capable of stealing, but she was here. Right where they expected the thief to show his—or her—face.

Millie threw her hands up. "I'm looking for you, of course. Why are you hiding in the laundry room in the middle of the night?"

Was it possible? Relief washed over Dora. Her fearful heart slowed, and she felt as if she'd stepped away from the edge of a deep canyon. "I . . . well . . ." Her mind went empty with any believable explanation.

Millie looked her roommate up and down. "If you were Penny or Adelaide, I'd surmise you were here to meet a man. But . . . " She trailed off as she watched Dora's face.

Dora didn't know what it was in her expression that might have given away her guilt at having met Jake in the parlor last night, but Millie caught it. In fact, Dora didn't know why she felt guilty at all. It was perfectly acceptable to sit in the parlor and converse, provided she wasn't alone with him. But she knew, in her heart, it was more than just conversation. And that must have been exactly what Millie saw.

Millie opened her mouth to speak just as Jake appeared behind her.

"Dora?" Jake reached past Millie and took Dora's hand. She was so stunned, she couldn't even think of words to say.

Millie glanced between the two of them and stepped back into the hall, letting Jake pull Dora closer to him.

"Please," Jake said to Millie. "I hope you'll find it in your heart to keep our feelings for each other to yourself." Remorse colored every aspect of his features. He continued to hold Dora's hand, his grip strong and warm. If Dora thought she couldn't find words before, the feel of his palm against hers and the way he'd laced his fingers between her own made her forget she'd ever known how to talk at all.

Millie crossed her arms even as her face softened. "I have no desire to see my friend lose her position here. All that concerns me is what sort of man you are."

"I promise I have only good intentions." Jake glanced at Dora, his eyes dark in the shadows of the hallway.

Dora was struck with the strangest urge to raise her free hand and trace her fingers along the sharp angle of his jaw. She tried to shove her hand into the pocket of her skirt, only to remember she was wearing a robe. Embarrassment flitted through her for a moment, quickly cut off when Jake began rubbing a tiny circle with his thumb on the back of the hand he held. Then all rational thought fled her mind once again.

"Every man says that." Millie narrowed her eyes at Jake. Millie's own experience with the horrible Mr. Turner, who'd used her affections to take control of the hotel's construction last summer, had made her wary of every man who crossed her path. Dora couldn't blame her for being suspicious, and if she had the ability to speak, she would have told Millie that Jake was nothing like Mr. Turner.

*Was he?* The thought sent alarm bells ringing throughout Dora's body. She stiffened, even as Jake continued to trace circles on her hand.

"I'm not every man," he said. "Dora captured my heart the first moment I saw her. I should never have asked her to meet me down here." He turned then to Dora, taking her other hand in his. "I promise never to put you in such a position again." Then he leaned forward and placed a kiss on her forehead, and the world spun.

She blinked at him, slowly nodding her assent only so Millie wouldn't discover the real reason they were here. But his words . . . She'd be foolish to believe them, despite the flirtatious manner he'd taken with her before. He'd only known her for a few days. These were lies, intended to convince Millie. But if they were, he was quite adept at it. Perhaps the attention he'd paid her before was a lie too. Then he gave her a wink, so quick she might've missed it if she blinked. What did that mean?

"All right," Millie said. "I have no choice but to trust you, Mr. James. Dora, I'll see you upstairs soon?"

"Soon." Dora choked out the word.

Millie nodded, then swept down the hallway.

Jake watched her go before turning back to Dora. But his usual smile was gone. "I told you not to come down here."

The haze that had clouded Dora's thoughts broke into a thousand pieces. She yanked her hands from his and took a step backward, only to knock into the doorframe. "I don't have to obey your orders," she snapped at him. Where that had come from, Dora didn't know. Perhaps she'd spent too much time in the company of girls like Penny and Millie. The words buzzed through her, making her hands shake. She clenched them into fists and shoved them into the folds of her robe.

"I didn't say that to order you around. I told you this could be dangerous. Did you think about what could've happened if the thief had shown himself?" Jake placed a hand against the wall next to the doorframe. "You could've been hurt. Or worse. And I—" He stopped, his face just inches from hers, and shook his head.

"And you . . .?" Dora's voice came out as a whisper. He was much too close. Even in the darkness she could see the dark stubble that dotted his chin. His warm breath tickled across her skin and his eyes roved across her face. She felt that if she even breathed differently, she'd find his lips pressed against hers. She swallowed and waited for him to answer.

"I can't bear for anything to happen to you," he finally said, his voice ragged. "It would break me."

Dora's heart contracted. It wasn't a lie, what he'd said to Millie.

He had feelings for her.

# Chapter Twelve

Perhaps he'd said too much, but Jacob couldn't keep it inside any longer. Dora's face softened, and it took every ounce of self-control he had not to kiss her. Even if she found it in her heart to care for him, he'd need to be careful with her. She certainly wasn't some debutante from New York, practiced in the art of attracting men like bees to honey.

Dora was different, and he liked that about her. So he stayed where he was—close, but not too close.

"I didn't mean to scare you," she said.

He closed his eyes a moment. He'd been harsh with her. "I apologize for reacting the way I did." He studied her face again, drinking in her big brown eyes, her olive skin, the shape of her nose. She was perfect, and she seemed to not realize it. As if it had a mind of its own, his hand found its way to her cheek, and he let it linger there as she closed her eyes and stiffened, just a little.

*Careful*, the sensible voice in his head warned. He pulled his hand away. It felt as if he'd just stepped from the warmth of a hearth into the frozen winter. How he wished he could place a hand on either side of her face and kiss away any doubts she might have about him.

"I had a friend in Chicago," he said, by way of not only explaining his reaction but also distracting himself from his own imagination. "His sister was almost like a sister to me, too. One evening at a party, she left the house with a man we didn't know. Only no one realized it until long after they'd left. We searched for her. I finally found her in an alley, and . . ." Jacob paused, taking in Dora's horrified expression. "He was after her money and jewelry. When she refused to give anything to him, he hurt her. I couldn't imagine you in such a situation. I know that doesn't excuse my behavior, but I hope it offers some explanation for it."

"That's awful," Dora said. "I'm so sorry for her and for your friend. It's a good thing you found her."

Jacob pushed aside the images that had returned from that night. "I'd never been so afraid in my life," he said.

"I can imagine. Your friends must have been quite well-to-do for her to be targeted in such a way."

Jacob's heart nearly stopped. He'd forgotten. Completely forgotten that he wasn't Jacob Gilbert here. He was Jake James, from a working-class family in Chicago. He felt so comfortable with Dora that he'd nearly let it slip. "They were," he said slowly, praying she wouldn't ask any other questions. How would he explain how he, as Jake, went to house parties with such people? How would he have met friends like that to begin with?

"I'm sorry to have scared you," she said.

He forced himself to breathe. "I'm sorry to have been so insistent on you remaining away from here. Perhaps we can come to an agreement that will satisfy both of us in the future."

She smiled a little at that, and Jacob's heart warmed, his misspoken words almost forgotten. "I'd like that." She paused, her smile growing. "You remind me some of a cousin I have."

"Oh?" She'd said so little about her family that Jake was immediately curious.

"Yes. He thought protecting me and his sisters was his responsibility and his alone. He would've done the same as you."

"How did he feel about you coming to work here?" Even though the hotel belonged to his family, Jacob didn't think he'd be thrilled if one of his own sisters wanted to work here. Despite the safety within the hotel, this was still very much the unsettled frontier. Why, just last month one of the waitresses had been kidnapped by an outlaw gang. His father had railed about that incident for nearly a week.

"He doesn't know." Dora cast her eyes down toward the floor.

"Where does he think you've gone?"

She shrugged her shoulders. "I'm not certain. My mother invented some story after I left."

"None of your family knows except your mother?" People of Jacob's social circles looked down on waitressing, or any other women's work, for that matter, but it surprised him that Dora's family would have been ashamed of her choice in work. Working in a Gilbert hotel was far more respectable than many other options.

She nodded. "It's safer that way."

"Safer?"

Her cheeks colored. "Better, I meant. It's better no one else knows."

Jacob eyed her for a moment, puzzling through her reaction. It made no sense, but then again, what did he know of her family? Despite their circumstances, perhaps she was expected to do as his own sisters were—marry and start their own families. "Do you like it here?"

She looked up at him again, that shy smile inching the corners of her lips up. "I do, very much."

"In that case, you should return to your room before anyone discovers you here."

She hesitated, and then reached for his hand. "Thank you for listening. This work means everything to me, and I couldn't bear for the hotel to run into problems because of this thief. My family relies on the money I send home."

"I . . ." Jacob cleared his throat, trying to wrest his mind away from the fact that *she* reached for his hand, not the other way around. Her grip was light, her small fingers wrapped warmly around his larger hand. If she let go, he feared he'd go chasing her down the hallway just to feel her hand on his again. "I enjoy hearing you speak."

She laughed, then dropped his hand before disappearing down the hall. He forced himself to remain in place.

*I enjoy hearing you speak*? What sort of response was that? This woman had made him go daft. Never in his life had Jacob Gilbert been unable to properly speak to a woman.

Not until he met Dora Reynolds.

# Chapter Thirteen

D ora hummed as she tied the strings of her apron into a bow. It was good fortune that she hadn't been scheduled to work the breakfast shift this morning, since she'd stayed up most of the night waiting for a thief who never came. But Jake had come to her rescue with Millie. . . and she couldn't stop thinking about him. That lilt in his grin, the way his eyes nearly danced when he smiled, how comforting and yet thrilling it had felt to have her hands in his, how tongue-tied he'd gotten when she took his hand herself. When she left the reservation, she'd never imagined meeting a man like Jake. All she'd planned to do was work, send money to her mother, and try to remain as inconspicuous as possible.

She hoped she wasn't inconspicuous to Jake, though.

She couldn't be, not with the way he sought her out and confided in her. The thought set her humming again as she redid the mess of a bow.

"I don't believe she knows we're here, much less understands what we're saying." Penny's voice infiltrated Dora's daydreams.

Dora turned and blinked at Penny and Millie. Millie hid her smile while Penny popped her hands on her hips, a piece of lace dangling from her fingers.

"I came in here to ask your opinion on whether the vases in the dining room would be prettier sitting on pieces of lace. But it looks as if you have far more important things on your mind," Penny said.

"I doubt Mrs. Ruby will let you redecorate her dining room just for your wedding luncheon," Millie said.

"Of course she will!" Penny looked aghast at Millie's words. Dora had to laugh. Penny had let her upcoming wedding overtake every other thought in her head. More than once, Dora and Millie had confided in each other how much they wished she was married already, if only to end the nonstop wedding talk.

"I believe you need to speak to Mrs. Ruby about working again," Dora said, fluffing the bow on her apron. "Then you might have something else to occupy your mind."

Penny gasped as if Dora had struck her. She turned to Millie, who nodded in assent. She turned back to say something to Dora, but then her face changed into a sly grin. "You, Dora Reynolds, are attempting to draw our attention away from you. And your . . ." She waved a hand at Dora's perfectly tied bow.

Millie crossed her arms. "I didn't tell you what I happened upon last night."

Penny's eyes widened. She sat on the edge of Millie's bed, hands pressed down onto the mattress. "I'm waiting."

Millie looked to Dora. "It's for her to tell, not me."

"Is this about why you wanted to sneak out of your room last night?" Penny asked.

"You knew about that?" Millie's jaw dropped.

Dora bit down on her lip to keep a sigh from escaping. She knew there would be no keeping of secrets from either of these two. Luckily, they were both such good friends to her that she knew they'd keep her confidence. And it might help her to speak her feelings out loud to girls she could trust.

The clock in the hallway chimed the quarter hour.

"I'll tell you both everything, but it will have to wait until later. Millie and I have work to do." Dora reached for her friend's hand, bid Penny goodbye, and walked quickly toward the stairs.

"I cannot wait to hear more about your gallant Mr. James," Millie whispered as they crossed the lobby.

Dora glanced at the front desk out of habit. Jake was there, helping a guest. "I promise I'll tell you tonight."

"Unless you're too busy meeting with him again." Millie batted her eyelashes at Dora.

When they entered the dining room, they found that Mrs. Ruby had called a meeting. This wasn't unusual. She generally used the time to alert the girls to changes in the menu or special guests onboard the incoming train. Sometimes she had accolades to give to those who had worked the hardest, or gentle reminders about etiquette and quickness. Today, though, Dora thought she looked somber.

Just as it appeared that all the girls for the lunch shift had arrived, Mr. Mc-Farland entered the dining room. Dora glanced at Millie, who looked back at her with wide eyes. This was highly unusual. Mr. McFarland only came to these meetings for particularly serious reasons. And Dora had a sneaking suspicion she knew exactly what that reason was. But how . . . ?

"Good morning, girls," Mrs. Ruby said, her voice booming across the dining room over the girls' chatter. Everyone instantly quieted down, and Mrs. Ruby lowered her voice. "I have a couple of announcements about today's lunch and dinner menus, but first, Mr. McFarland is here to speak to you about something very serious." She nodded at Mr. McFarland, who stepped forward, his hands resting on his broad stomach.

"I'm sorry to say that I'm here with some bad news," he said in his lingering Irish accent.

Dora twisted her hands into her skirts, knowing exactly what he was about to say. It was the *how* of it that still puzzled her.

"Last night, more of the hotel's funds went missing. A significant amount." He eyed them one at a time, down the line. "We've had no guests that have been at the hotel so long as to be responsible for these thefts, and I'm sorry to say that at this point, we suspect the thief is one of our own employees. I implore you to keep your eyes and ears open. If you notice anything—anything at all—that appears out of the ordinary, please tell myself or Mrs. Ruby immediately."

Dora's mind spun. How had the thief managed to steal the money when both she and Jake were in that hallway last night? It was possible it had happened earlier, before they arrived. But that would have been too risky. Employees and guests were often awake and about until late. The culprit could have been caught too easily. And the only person Dora or Jake had seen all night was Millie. If Jake had seen someone else after Dora returned upstairs, surely he would have told her.

She glanced at her friend, whose eyes were on Mr. McFarland. Millie wouldn't do such a thing, despite the mistakes she had made when she first arrived in Crest Stone. Besides, when would she have stolen the money? She'd come down that hallway and immediately found Dora, and then left. Dora and Jake had been there a while longer, but Millie was asleep in bed when Dora returned. It was impossible.

"The company cannot keep an unprofitable hotel afloat for too long," Mr. McFarland was saying. "If the Crest Stone continues to lose money, I fear we will not be open much longer."

Several of the girls gasped while others began speaking to each other in concerned tones. Dora said nothing, but her heart fell into her shoes. The hotel *couldn't* close. She needed this work too much. It had taken every bit of strength she had to procure a position here. She couldn't imagine needing to do it all again. And what would she do without Millie or Penny, or Caroline who lived nearby? And what about Jake?

They had to find the thief. That was the only answer. And they had to do it soon.

# Chapter Fourteen

Jake trudged through the snow in the darkness, with only a sliver of a moon and a mess of stars obscured by clouds barely lighting the sky. He'd felt the rare need to be away from people so he could think. Of course, now that he couldn't feel his fingers, he debated whether going outside to do this was the wisest course of action.

But he needed to think through what had happened last night. More money had disappeared, and he could *not* pinpoint how. And then, of course, there was Dora. He'd spent his walk bouncing between distress and elation. Surely this mess of emotions couldn't be good for one's health.

"Jake!"

His name on her voice was like bells through the frozen air. What he wouldn't give to hear her say his given name. He stopped and turned to meet her.

Dora's breath came quick after she hurried through the snow to him. Her face was flushed with the cold, but her eyes shone in the little light that came from above. She reminded him of an angel from a Christmas pageant. Despite all his worries, he couldn't keep the smile off his face.

"It's far too cold out here for conversation," he said. He wanted to take her hand, but didn't dare. Anyone could be peering through the dining-room windows or those from the guest rooms on the second floor. "The stablehands are at their dinner, where I imagine they'll remain for as long as possible. Why don't I meet you in the stables?"

Dora glanced back at the hotel, then nodded. The moment she headed toward the stables, he strode in the direction of the creek. After sufficient time had passed—and after he was certain he'd never have feeling in his fingertips again—Jacob doubled back and entered the stables from a door on the south side, far from the prying eyes of the hotel.

He found Dora lighting one of the lamps that hung from a nail on the wall. "I'm glad you sought me out," he said, standing just inside the door.

Dora turned to face him, the flame from the lamp dancing across her features. "Mrs. Ruby informed us earlier that more money has gone missing."

"McFarland held a meeting with the desk staff and the bellhops this morning." Jacob flexed his fingers, trying to revive the warmth in his hands. He could bear the pungent smell of the stables if he could just work some feeling back into his fingers and toes. "We missed something—someone—last night."

"I don't understand how," Dora replied. "We were there most of the night, unless the thief took his chances earlier or later."

"It's unlikely." Jacob stepped around the spindly chairs that were set up with a little table. Straw crunched under his boots.

"It's the only explanation."

Jacob nodded. "I've thought about it all day, and I came to the same conclusion."

"What do we do now?" Dora placed a hand around one of the posts holding up the ceiling of the stables. Somewhere nearby, a horse shuffled and huffed.

"I don't know," Jacob said, honestly. In all his thinking, he couldn't decide upon a plan of action. The fear of failure nipped at the edges of his mind, and it took all he had to keep it at bay. "It may be time to bring McFarland into my confidence. I highly doubt he's the culprit."

"The McFarlands would never steal from the hotel," Dora said.

"Anyone would steal, given the right motive and opportunity."

Dora frowned. "I don't believe that. I imagine most people are honest and loyal, and would never fall to such levels."

Her words were a sweet mountain breeze in the manure-and-straw air. How had she come to be so trusting? She was like no other woman he'd met. Girls from the city were usually skeptical and shrewd, not starry-eyed and full of hope, like his Dora.

*His Dora.* How he wished that were true. She watched him now, those big eyes the same color as night, her face reflecting every good thing that existed in the world. He grabbed on to the same post she held to keep from sweeping her up into his arms.

"Jake?" she said, her voice much less confident than when professing her belief in the goodness of all mankind.

"Yes?"

"I know you've mentioned it before, but do you truly believe Mr. McFarland was correct in saying the hotel won't remain open if these thefts continue?" She cast her eyes downward, toward the straw-covered dirt floor.

"Unfortunately, yes. The Gilbert Company prefers to make a profit. It's never happened before, but Mr. Gilbert wouldn't hesitate if it meant he'd stop losing money."

She lifted her head. "How do you know such things?"

"Mr. Gilbert told me when he hired me to investigate." The partial lie tripped off his tongue. His father certainly had told him, and he was being paid to investigate. But the whole of the statement rang false in Jacob's mind. And he realized, at that moment, that he despised keeping the secret of who he was from Dora. The future came hurtling toward him. He'd leave here at some point, his investigation either concluded or handed over to Pinkertons. What then? Would he confess his true identity to Dora and hope she forgave him? Or would he leave her here, never to speak to her again? The first option terrified him, but the latter threatened to shatter his heart entirely.

She watched him now, her eyes narrowed just so. For half a moment, he feared she'd figured him out. But then she looked away, back toward the rear of the stables.

"Dora?" he said gently when she didn't turn back to him.

Her chest rose and fell as she breathed, but she said nothing. And she didn't look at him. Something was wrong.

Jacob took a couple of steps around her until he was in her line of vision again. She quickly looked back the other way, but not before he saw the tears swimming in her eyes.

"What's wrong? Did something happen?" He took a cautious step toward her. When she didn't move, he placed a hand on her elbow.

She sniffled but still didn't look at him, as if she were embarrassed to let him see her tears. "Nothing happened," she finally said. "It's only . . . what might be. The Crest Stone can't be closed."

"We're trying not to let that happen," he said, keeping his hand on her elbow.

"I know. But what if we don't succeed? If the hotel closes, I'll have no position. My family . . ." She choked as a sob shook her body. She raised a hand to cover her mouth.

"Shh." Jacob pulled her to him.

Dora didn't protest. Instead, she let him hold her and leaned her face against his chest. He rubbed her back, and her tears dampened his coat. When she seemed to quiet some, he spoke. "The Gilbert Company would ensure that each of the employees here has work in a different hotel. You don't need to fear that."

She sniffed again, and he could feel her nodding against his chest. "It wouldn't be the same," she finally said.

"No," he replied. "I suppose it wouldn't." The Crest Stone Hotel and Restaurant was a special place. Jacob had been here for less than a week, and that was already clear to him. And it wasn't just the beautiful, remote mountain valley—it was the people who worked here. It would be a shame to see this hotel shuttered.

He leaned his face down into her hair. She smelled of fresh air and wildflowers. How she could smell of wildflowers in December was beyond him, but he couldn't get enough of the scent. "I promise you I'll do everything I can to keep that from happening."

She pulled back just a little, but remained in his arms. She drew a hand across her face, wiping away the tears that remained. "How are you so confident?"

He laughed a little, a throaty, guttural sound. "I suppose it was how I was raised," he finally said.

"Your family must be quite different from mine. I . . . I'd like to meet them someday." Then, as if she'd just understood what she said, she ducked her head.

"I'd like that." It was the most honest thing he'd said since he'd arrived here in Crest Stone.

Her chin rose as she looked back up at him, a shy smile making its way across her face. His heart pounded in his ears, drowning out any sound of horses or his own sense. He moved one of his hands up to the back of her neck. It didn't matter who his family was or why he was here. Nothing mattered in this moment but Dora in his arms.

He lowered his face toward hers and her eyes fluttered shut. Her breath on his face was warm and quick. All he wanted to do with his life was keep her safe and happy. Starting right now. His lips touched hers and—

A blast of cold air hit him as the door to the stable flew open.

# Chapter Fifteen

Dora stumbled backward in a daze. One moment, she was drowning in Jake's embrace, and now she was alone, searching for her bearings and trying to piece together what had just happened. Her fingers flew to her lips. Jake hadn't kissed her, had he? No, because someone had interrupted them.

*Someone.*

Dora thought she might be sick. The door to the stables had shut, taking with it the freezing air that had blown in. Dora blinked in the gloom, trying to see who had come in.

"Oh, I'm—I'm sorry," a quiet voice said.

Dora squinted, barely making out the woman's shape. The woman stepped forward, light from the single lamp glinting off spectacles perched on her nose.

Edie. Dora took a deep breath. She barely knew the girl. And she certainly didn't know if Edie was the sort who kept confidences or who went running to gossip or—worse—share what she'd seen with Mrs. Ruby. It was one thing to talk about finding a man attractive, and something else to be found in his embrace.

"I didn't mean to interrupt your conversation," Edie said, her hands clasped in front of her. "I was looking for the stablehands. To let them know to come for supper."

*Conversation.* The word whirled through Dora's head. Did that mean Edie hadn't seen Jake about to kiss her? Edie looked earnest, not as if she'd just trapped a beaver.

"What a coincidence," Jake said from where he stood, now several feet away. "D—Miss Reynolds here had just arrived to do the same."

She had? Dora forced her face to maintain a pleasant look, despite Jake's lie for her. Never had she been asked to fetch anyone for supper. It must be a regular chore for Edie. But coming all the way out here in the cold? It seemed work better suited for one of the kitchen boys.

"And as I told her, your invitation comes too late. The stablehands are already at their supper in the kitchen. And now that I've brought leftover turnips and carrots for the horses, I must be on my way. I bid you ladies good evening." He tugged at his hat, and as soon as Edie turned away, he raised his eyebrows at Dora in a silent question.

She nodded just slightly. She'd be fine here with Edie, who seemed to be oblivious to what had just happened. Dora knew she should be thankful, but for now, it took everything she had just to act normal.

"Shall we return together?" Edie asked.

Dora nodded and pulled her hood up to cover her head. "Do you often have to fetch the stablehands for dinner?" she asked as they secured the stable door behind them. Tiny snowflakes swirled through the air, biting at her face.

"Not often," Edie replied, tugging her own hood up. "Do you?"

"No." At least that was the truth. "Perhaps everyone is concerned they'll starve in this weather."

Edie laughed, but it sounded forced. "Perhaps."

They walked the rest of the way in silence. Dora's mind flitted between Jake and the missing money. They entered the hotel through the back door that led down the hallway to the kitchen, the ladies' parlor, and eventually, the lobby.

Edie stopped at the kitchen door. "I want to ensure they're in here."

"Thank you for looking," Dora said. "Else we'll both be in trouble." As soon as Edie disappeared through the door, Dora hoped that was the last falsehood she'd need to rely on, at least for one night.

She wandered through the lobby, glancing out of habit at the front desk. Jake was nowhere to be seen. Dora eased her way through the guests gathered near the fireplace. She passed the stairs and stood instead in the hallway that led back to the hotel office and the laundry room. Something bothered her about last night, but she couldn't quite remember what it was. Standing here didn't serve her memory at all. At least not for the elusive thought she'd hoped to remember.

Instead, she remembered Jake. Jake's hand on the back of her neck, warm and reassuring. His eyes, seeking out her true self. His lips—

She squeezed her eyes shut at the memory. Why had she let him take such liberties? It wouldn't end well. It couldn't. She couldn't go on pretending she wasn't who she was, not if they carried on this way. She'd need to tell him about her family. About how horrible it was being moved to the reservation after they'd followed in the footsteps of generations of their ancestors, traveling with the seasons through these mountains, into the valleys, following game as the weather allowed. About the traditions she missed so deeply they cut grooves through her heart—the horse races, the Sun Dance, seeing distant relatives and friends at trading gatherings. About how as much as she loved the hotel and her friends here, a part of her would always be missing as she pretended to be Dora from Chicago. About the guilt she felt daily as she did her work, even though she knew what she did was the only way her family could survive.

What would he think about all of that? Would he still look at her the same way? Or would he be appalled? Angry that she wasn't honest with him?

And what would she do if they couldn't catch the thief? Jake had said Dora and the other girls could get work at another Gilbert hotel dining room, but how did he know that for certain? It didn't seem as if he'd worked for the company long enough to be privy to such information. Besides, Dora didn't know how she could survive being even farther away from her family. At least from here, they were but a few days' ride away to the southwest. If she closed her eyes at night and cleared her mind, it was almost as if she could feel their presence. How could she sense them if she needed to relocate to some other hotel in, say, Montana or California? But if she didn't go, her family would . . . She couldn't even think the words.

Tears pricked Dora's eyes for the second time in a day. Two of the maids left the laundry room at the end of the hall, and Dora quickly swiped her hand across her eyes.

"No need for ironing today!" Helen said as she and another girl passed Dora. "Georgie and I have already taken care of it."

Dora nodded, pasting a smile on her face. They disappeared, only to be replaced by Mrs. McFarland, leaving the hotel office. She took care to lock the door before walking quickly toward Dora and the lobby.

"Good evening, my dear," she said as she approached Dora. She paused, her gaze taking in Dora's face. "Is everything all right?"

"It is, thank you," Dora said. "I . . . well, I worry. About the hotel and what will happen . . ." That certainly wasn't a lie. The fear had eaten away at the edges of her mind all day.

Mrs. McFarland laid a hand on Dora's arm. "I worry, too. But we aren't to that point yet, so worrying is but a useless activity that only serves to distract us."

Dora gave her a little smile. "That is true. Do you know anything more yet?"

"Not yet. The money seems to be disappearing overnight. I've taken to doing the books twice a day now, and it's always morning when I discover the missing funds. I've never seen such a thing. Not even when I ran my brother's ranch, and there was certainly opportunity there for someone to steal money from us."

"I hope we can uncover the thief soon," Dora said.

"As do I. Now, it's late. You should get on upstairs before Mrs. Ruby comes searching for you." Mrs. McFarland squeezed Dora's arm before retracing her steps to the apartment she shared with her husband. She nodded at Dora before disappearing inside.

Dora sighed and gathered up her skirts to climb the stairs. She resolved to listen and watch even harder than she had been. They had to uncover this thief before it was too late.

# Chapter Sixteen

Jacob knocked on the door to the hotel office. After a moment, it opened to McFarland on the other side. He let Jacob enter before shutting the door again. The large room held two desks, one for McFarland and the other for his wife, who was there now, her lips moving silently as she ran a finger down a column in a large ledger. Stacks of bills sat upon her desk, along with a few papers and envelopes.

"Thank you for seeing me," he said to McFarland, who eyed him watching his wife with the money. Jacob knew immediately what the man thought. Luckily, he could dispel his worries. "Could I speak to you alone?"

McFarland glanced at his wife, who nodded, and then led the way out the door. They walked a short way down the hall before stopping at a door near the stairs. McFarland unlocked it and held it open for Jacob to enter.

"These are our rooms," McFarland said by way of explanation. "Please, sit."

Jacob took a seat in an armchair. The apartment appeared small but comfortable. It was certainly more home-like than a hotel room or Jacob's room in the men's dormitory upstairs. "Thank you, sir."

McFarland settled himself in a chair across from Jacob. "Now, pray tell, what's on your mind that requires such privacy, Mr. James?"

Jacob took a deep breath and leaned forward. Being direct was the best route to take here. "My name is not Jake James. It's Jacob Gilbert. I'm here on request of my father, James Gilbert, Sr., to see if I can't find this thief before the company calls in the Pinkerton Agency."

If McFarland was surprised at all at his words, he didn't show it. Instead, he leaned back in his chair and stroked his beard. "Well. Now there's a revelation. And how do I know you speak the truth? I must be skeptical, as you can imagine."

Jacob expected no less. He came prepared for just such a question, and reached into the pocket of his vest to extract the telegrams sent from Denver. He passed them to McFarland, who studied them closely before returning them to Jacob.

"Might I ask why you're just coming to me now with this information?" McFarland said.

"I had to make certain you were not the embezzler. Sir," Jacob added, hoping to soften his words. "I hope you understand."

McFarland nodded. "Yes. Yes, I suppose I do. Now, do I get to be privy to your investigation to date?" The man still sounded a bit irritated. It made sense, after all. Jacob supposed he would feel the same if he were in McFarland's place.

"So far, I have nothing. The only people I've ruled out are you and your wife. I was hoping we could collaborate."

McFarland sat forward. "That would be for the best. What do you have in mind?"

"It's clear the money is disappearing from the safe overnight. I attempted to set up a watch a few evenings ago, but I must have either arrived too late or left too early, because we—I—never laid eyes on the thief. I propose we set up another watch, this time covering the office door from the moment you leave for the evening until the moment you arrive in the morning." Jacob stopped, hoping McFarland didn't notice his slip. There was no need to share the fact he'd worked with Dora on the investigation, particularly since it might cause her to lose her position here. Not to mention, McFarland wouldn't take kindly to the knowledge that one of his waitresses knew *why* Jacob was here before he did, even if she didn't know his true identity.

"The company is sending an emergency shipment of funds. It's due to arrive tomorrow," McFarland said. "We generally keep the arrival of money quiet, as you can imagine, but perhaps we can make this one a bit . . . less quiet, to draw out the thief."

"Excellent." It was similar to the plan Jacob had executed with Dora, except this time, there was an actual shipment of money. It had certainly worked then as more money had gone missing; there was no reason it shouldn't work again.

Except this time, they'd catch the culprit.

JACOB ARRIVED TO THE kitchen early for breakfast the next morning, hoping to find Dora. She was there not even a minute later, dressed in her gray and white Gilbert Company dress and apron, her midnight hair neatly pulled back under a white cap. She looked radiant, even dressed the same as every other girl who worked in the dining room.

Something clattered to the floor. The bellhop behind Jacob tapped him on the shoulder and handed him a fork. "You dropped this."

"Thanks." He could've dropped his entire plate of food and not noticed, thanks to the beauty that had drawn all his attention entirely onto her. Jacob exchanged the fork for a clean one, after apologizing to the boy washing dishes, and then found a seat across from Dora.

She snuck a glance up at him when he sat. "Good morning," she said cordially. They were surrounded with other waitresses, bellhops, handymen, desk clerks, maids, and even a few kitchen boys, rushing to eat a small breakfast before they were needed in earnest.

"Good morning, Miss Reynolds," he replied. He let his eyes linger a moment on hers, sharing a smile that was meant for her and her alone.

She smiled back. She didn't need to say any words. They'd had an entire conversation with just the expressions on their faces, and no one was the wiser.

He finished his meal first and waited for her to eat the remainder of her eggs. When she did, he stood and collected both their plates and cups. "I'll take these." He reached for her napkin and deftly dropped a folded-up scrap of paper into her lap. He paused for just a moment to ensure she'd seen it, and then returned the dirty dishes.

Jacob caught Dora's eye as she stood from the bench. She nodded at him, so quick no one else would notice, and then smiled, seemingly to herself. He stepped out of the kitchen through the hallway door, and then headed toward the lobby. Dora's smile had been exactly what he'd hoped for with that note. It might have been a foolhardy thing, inviting her to join himself and McFarland tonight, albeit from the laundry room, where McFarland wouldn't know she was there. But he trusted her to remain safe, hidden and out of the way. She deserved to see them catch the thief.

This evening couldn't arrive soon enough. He was ready to put an end to this matter.

And then he could worry about how to tell Dora the truth about his identity.

# Chapter Seventeen

Dora woke with a start. She blinked a moment, wondering where she was and why her neck hurt so badly. The room came into focus, shadowy from just the little moonlight streaming through the window. Dora rubbed her neck. She was seated in a chair in the laundry room, right up against the door.

Stifling a yawn, she pushed the door open a crack. The hallway was empty. A couple of doors down, she could make out one of the hotel room doors, also likely opened just a sliver. Jake and Mr. McFarland kept watch there.

Dora closed her door. It was imperative that Mr. McFarland not know she was here. Jake's note had been brief, but clear—she was invited to wait here for the thief, but she must remain in this room, unseen and safe. She didn't mind. After all, she had no desire to confront the man who was stealing from the hotel. And she certainly didn't wish Mr. McFarland to know she'd been spending time alone with Jake.

She stretched and wondered at the time. And she hoped Millie didn't awaken and come looking for her again. She shouldn't—not now that she thought she knew why Dora had crept out of their room before.

The minutes ticked by, and Dora fought to keep her eyes open. She didn't want to miss the moment the thief was finally caught. But sleep was hard to keep at bay. Her eyes closed, and she promised herself it was just for a moment.

A door shut, so softly Dora wouldn't have heard it if she hadn't been right next to it. Her eyes flew open. Was it real? Or had she started dreaming? Her heart hammered in her chest, and she swallowed before peering through the crack in the laundry room door.

It was real. A figure had entered the hallway from the outside door—the one that was located just to the right of the laundry room where Dora sat. Dora didn't dare breathe as the person walked slowly and silently by her door. It was a woman, that much was clear from the dress and the coat. Her hair was obscured under a hood.

The figure stopped at the office door. Dora gasped and then threw a hand over her mouth. But it didn't seem as though the woman had heard. Dora forced herself to breathe normally. This must be the thief.

The woman stood there a moment, patting the side of her coat. Then she turned away from Dora. Another minute passed. Dora strained to see what the woman was doing, but it was no use. All at once, the mystery woman turned and retraced her steps back to the outside door. Her head was turned, so Dora was unable to catch a glimpse of her face. The woman slipped the door open and slid out, quiet as the valley on a snow-covered morning.

Dora turned to look back down the hallway, waiting for the men to emerge and follow this strange woman outside. A few seconds passed. Then a few more. She was going to escape if no one went after her now. Perhaps the men had fallen asleep.

Not giving herself even the tiniest portion of a moment to consider the potential danger, Dora eased the laundry door open and followed the woman's steps. The air outside was still, thankfully, but snowflakes drifted down, lazy and unaware that a thief was making her way through their midst. Dora rubbed her hands up and down her arms. She couldn't stay out here long without a coat, but hopefully it wouldn't take long to track down the woman she'd seen. What she wouldn't give for a rabbit fur coat and a pair of sensible boots right now.

Footsteps in the new-fallen snow led to the right, through the garden and around the north wing of the hotel. Dora hurried after them, thankful for even the little bit of moon that illuminated them for her. She followed the trail past the north wing and around the front of the hotel. Just as she started down the hill, she saw a figure crossing the railroad tracks.

Snow-soaked shoes and frozen fingers forgotten, Dora picked up her pace, running to catch up with the woman. Past the tracks, not too far from the house where Caroline and her husband lived and ran the mercantile, the woman stopped.

Dora nearly tripped over the railroad tracks. Why had she stopped instead of running faster? Was it a trick? Dora slowed down, wary now. She had no way to defend herself if she needed to. This had been foolish, coming out here to chase a desperate person. She should've gone to Jake and Mr. McFarland and taken her chances with getting into trouble.

But it was too late for that now. She had two choices—continue forward and discover who this thief was, or turn and run back to the hotel, hoping the woman wouldn't come after her.

Dora drew in a shuddering breath. And took a step forward.

It wasn't long before she drew even with the thief. The woman looked up at her, and Dora stopped in her tracks. Red hair curled out from under the woman's hood, and sharp eyes, still the lightest of blues even in the darkness, peered out at her.

"What are you doing out here?" Millie demanded.

Dora blinked at her. Millie wasn't the thief. She couldn't be. But what was she doing outside the office door in the dead of night? And what was she doing now? Dora's mind reeled back to the first night she and Jake had kept watch in the office hallway. Millie had appeared that night too. The thought *had* crossed Dora's mind then, and she'd explained it away. But now . . . it was far too much to be coincidental.

"What are *you* doing out here?" Dora turned the question back to Millie, drawing upon the strength of all her ancestors for courage.

Her friend's eyes widened at Dora's insistent question. Dora couldn't blame her. It wasn't as if Dora spoke up in such a demanding way all that often.

"It's . . ." Millie's gaze cast about the valley, almost as if she were expecting an answer to come rolling down the tracks from Cañon City. "It's a man, all right?"

"Is that wise? After what you went through with Mr. Turner?" Dora asked. Millie certainly hadn't mentioned any man lately.

Millie shuddered. "I've learned my lesson about horrible men. This one . . . he's very kind and polite."

"Mmm," Dora said. She crossed her arms tighter around herself. "I saw you come in. Why did you go back outside?"

"I've lost the key to our room." Millie patted the pocket of her skirt. "It's probably hopeless, trying to find it in this snow, but I thought I'd try before waking you up. Of course, it appears you were already awake . . ." She gave Dora a little, knowing smile.

Dora let the words hang in the air. Let Millie assume what she wanted, so long as she didn't suspect Dora had been lying in wait for the thief. "Come, let's get back to our room."

"I'll meet you there," Millie said. "I want to see if my key fell out of my pocket in the shanty."

Dora glanced over Millie's shoulder at the old railroad shanty that had served as the McFarlands' home before the hotel had been built. She nodded, unsure of what to believe, and then began retracing her steps to the hotel. She itched to tell Jake immediately about Millie, but she knew she couldn't wake him with Mr. McFarland there. It would have to wait until morning.

It seemed impossible that Millie was telling the truth. If there was a man, she would've told Dora and Penny before now. And that meant she must be the thief. But how could Millie do such a thing? Certainly, she'd made poor decisions when she first arrived in Crest Stone. But ever since then, she'd been such a good friend to Dora, to Penny, and to everyone else. Perhaps her family was in trouble. She never spoke of her family, but it was plausible. Believing Millie had a desperate reason to steal from the hotel didn't make it right, but it at least allowed Dora to feel sorry for her.

As soon as she arrived back into their room, Dora lit a lamp. She ignored the urge to peel off her soaking wet shoes and stockings, and instead began searching. If Millie had stolen so much money, it had to be here somewhere. Unless she'd already sent it away. Dora searched as long as she felt was safe, opening drawers, checking pockets in skirts, and even feeling underneath Millie's mattress.

But she turned up nothing.

It didn't matter. Evidence would have been nice, but the thief would strike again. Dora could only be grateful that something had stopped her tonight. She'd tell Jake in the morning, and together, they'd figure out a way to stop Millie.

# Chapter Eighteen

With the arrival of dawn, Jacob had awoken with a start. Furious with himself for falling asleep, he'd shaken McFarland awake. These late nights were taking a toll on him. He'd never catch the thief if he couldn't stay awake and watch. With dread curling in his stomach, he'd followed McFarland to the office where the hotel manager opened the safe and counted the money.

Three hundred dollars had gone missing overnight.

And after McFarland had left to return to his rooms, Jacob had been unable to find Dora. An ugly thought curled like smoke deep inside him. He refused to give it purchase. But it was impossible to ignore.

Dora had been there, both times.

Dora's family was poor.

He stopped on his way to the kitchen, squeezing his eyes shut and forcing the terrible thoughts away. He'd find her at breakfast and prove those suspicions wrong. Resolve renewed, he strode across the lobby and down the south wing hallway to the kitchen door.

Jacob didn't have to wait long. She arrived in the company of her red-haired friend, who was regaling her with some story. But Dora appeared to be distracted, casting her eyes about the room until they landed on Jacob. He hadn't even bothered to get a plate yet. Instead, he nodded at her and then tilted his head ever so slightly at the door that led outside. Dora gave him a quick nod in return.

He slipped out the door and waited not too far away, by the side of the smokehouse. It was a clear, cold morning. But despite the chill, Jacob didn't so much as shiver. He was too worried to think about anything beyond what he'd say to Dora. About five minutes later, she appeared, wearing a borrowed coat. She spotted him and gathered her skirts and coat to make her way across the snow to him.

"I suspect I know who the thief is," she said, just a little out of breath when she reached him.

Jacob raised his eyebrows. Dare he hope she had evidence to prove his suspicions wrong? "You do?"

"Yes!" Her cheeks flushed red from the cold, but her dark eyes sparkled like the sun on the snow. "I saw a woman in the hallway last night. She stopped for a long time by the office door, and then left to go outside again. I waited for you and Mr. McFarland to follow her. But when you didn't, I did."

Jacob closed his eyes briefly. Had they stayed awake, he might know whether Dora spoke the truth right now. If she was telling the truth, she'd put herself in danger. "That wasn't particularly smart," he said.

She frowned at him. "I *waited*. What else was I supposed to do? Let her leave unidentified? Or should I have woken you and let Mr. McFarland know we've been working together? And yes, I supposed you'd both fallen asleep."

Sheepish, Jacob nodded at her. "Please continue."

"Thank you." She twisted her bare hands together in front of her as she went on. "I followed her all the way across the tracks when she heard me. And when she turned around . . . it was Millie." When Jacob showed no sign of recognizing the name, she added, "My friend and roommate. The one I came down with this morning. Red hair?"

"Ah. And what did she have to say for herself?"

"She said she was meeting a man. Which . . . isn't unlike her. But, it's strange, really. She hadn't mentioned him before, and Millie's hardly shy about that sort of thing. But then again . . ." Dora broke off. "I don't want to believe she would steal from the hotel, but this is the second time she's been in that hallway when we were waiting for the thief to arrive. She stopped by the office door, and while she claimed she'd lost her key to our room, I wonder if it wasn't a key to the office she'd lost. And she's mentioned wishing she had more money . . ."

"It's plausible," Jacob said, his mind turning in about six different directions. "But she left without entering the office, correct?"

Dora nodded.

He pressed his lips together. Dora's friend couldn't be the thief. "Then she left without taking anything last night, right?"

"I suppose so."

"Yet this morning, McFarland discovered three hundred dollars missing from the safe." He crossed his arms and waited for her reaction.

Her eyes widened just a little and she balled her hands up. "How did that happen?"

"I don't know," he said honestly. "But I doubt it's your friend." He let that sink in for a moment before continuing. "I believe it's someone who desperately needs the money. Whether it's for family or to pay off some sort of debt, I don't think the thief continues stealing just to pad his—or her—own pockets."

"I imagine you're right," Dora said.

"Poverty is no good reason to steal. It's much better to rely on the generosity of one's friends and neighbors."

Dora studied him a moment. Perhaps he'd pushed too far.

"Yes, I agree," she finally said. "But to be fair, some people don't have friends or neighbors capable of helping in such a way."

"Then help can be found at benevolent societies and churches."

Dora tilted her head. "Those sorts of things don't exist in all places. What does this have to do with identifying the thief? Or are we attempting to discern the person's motives?"

He'd gone too far. "I'll discuss the situation with McFarland and let you know what our next steps will be."

"All right." She stood there, a dark-haired angel against the bright white of the snow, waiting. For him to show some sign of affection, or to say something that would make her laugh or blush.

But he couldn't. He wanted to, so badly he could almost feel the soft skin of her cheek against his fingers. He clenched them to his palms. "I bid you good morning, then."

Jacob left and returned to the kitchen without looking back. He filled a plate with food he knew he wouldn't be able to taste and tried to ignore the feeling that he'd sunk a knife into the depths of his heart.

*What if she wasn't the thief?* It was possible. But he had no suspects beyond Dora. He supposed it was plausible that her friend had later found the key and returned to steal the money while he and McFarland slept, but that would have been awfully brazen after Dora had discovered her.

And what did it mean when she said churches and benevolent societies didn't exist in all places? Certainly, no such thing could be found in this valley, but they were plentiful in cities like Chicago. Was she trying to deflect attention away from herself? Was she simply stating a fact because she wasn't the thief after all? Or was it something else entirely?

He shoved his plate aside, just as she returned to the kitchen. She didn't so much as glance his way. Her lack of attention was another arrow to his frayed emotions, but it was for the best.

Jacob returned his full plate and undrunk mug of coffee and made his way toward the front desk. He'd figure this mystery out if it was the last thing he did.

And he prayed Dora would be exonerated.

# Chapter Nineteen

Dora went through the motions of eating breakfast and serving the hotel's guests. She felt hollowed out, like a dead tree alone on a mountainside. It was only after her lunch shift was over that she shut herself in her room alone, thankful that Millie had work to do that afternoon, and let herself think.

Of course, the first thing she did the second the door shut wasn't thinking at all. Tears had been threatening to fall ever since Jake had turned away from her without even a glance that morning. He'd left her alone in the snow, confused and with the distinct feeling that he suspected her of stealing the money.

How was that possible? What about her character indicated she was anything less than honest?

*You aren't honest.* Dora sank into the chair that sat before the vanity table she and Millie shared. She wrapped her arms around herself, but no tears came. She was more angry than sad. Even if she did need to pretend to be someone she wasn't, that didn't mean he should presume she was a thief.

But did he? Dora stared at the wood floor. He'd dismissed her suspicions of Millie. And then he acted as if he thought Dora might be the culprit, but he never really said such a thing. Was she reading too much into it?

She stood and walked to the window, which looked out over the snow-covered land to the northeast. The railroad tracks cut through to the right, leading ever northward and southward. Beyond that, nothing but the occasional hill and tree broke the view toward the shadowy Wet Mountains to the east. There they stood, ancient, silent witnesses to her people's greatest triumphs and their worst tribulations.

Dora closed her eyes and tried to imagine this valley as it stood hundreds of years earlier, when the Ute came and went as they pleased. If no one had ever disturbed them, then perhaps she wouldn't be in the predicament she was in now. Instead, she'd be with her mother, helping her prepare a meal or trading stories and jokes with her cousins. Her mother never would have met her father, a white man Dora knew nothing of except the very little her mother had told her. Perhaps then Dora might have a good father, a proud man of the Muache band who kept his promises and loved his family.

She'd never have met Jake.

Despite the coldness he'd shown toward her that morning, the very thought of never having met him made her heart ache. Dora pressed her hands against the freezing window, letting the cold seep into her bones until the ache diminished and the frigid, hard truth crystallized in her mind.

She'd come here on her own, determined to do what she could to earn money for her mother, her aunts and uncles, her grandparents, her cousins. Without her, they'd starve. Her family was her priority, and she needed to remember that. She'd been foolish to trust a man like Jake. If her own father had shown her anything by leaving his marriage and family before she could walk, it was that men were not to be trusted with one's heart. Dora had known that, and yet she'd let down her guard and allowed Jake in. And where had that gotten her? It was even more foolish to believe he'd still care for her once he learned she wasn't who she'd presented herself to be.

Dora tapped a finger on the glass, melting the frost that had accumulated on the other side. If she was honest with herself, she'd also admit something about their conversation earlier had unsettled her—something beyond his coolness toward her and beyond him acting as if she were the thief. Dora couldn't quite grab hold of it, though. It was . . .

She chewed on her lower lip and left the window, pacing the small room until she came to the door, and then back again, dropping onto her bed. It was strange, but the feeling she'd gotten was that he was judging people—the thief, really, but it had felt broader than that—for being poor.

Now that she'd placed it in words, Dora almost laughed. It sounded ridiculous. It was almost as if she was imagining him coming from a well-to-do family, and not a policeman's home. Perhaps it was simply the company he'd kept. After all, he'd somehow befriended that wealthy man and his sister, the one he'd rescued from a thief in the alley.

All the more reason for her to keep her distance from him. If those were the sort of people he preferred to befriend, he would never understand her circumstances.

Dora stood and walked to the vanity table, where she sat and examined herself in the small, handheld mirror. Her eyes were red-rimmed, but that would pass after some time. She unpinned her hair, brushed it out, and repinned it, her mind made up.

She'd give all her attention to what was important—finding the thief so the hotel could remain open and she could keep her position here. She'd figure out once and for all if Millie was the culprit. Nothing would make her happier than to exonerate her friend, but she needed to find out for certain. As soon as she finished her hair, she pinched some color into her cheeks and then stood, casting her gaze about the room.

She'd make a thorough search of their room again. If that turned up nothing, she'd decide what to do next.

And—most important—she'd keep her distance from Jake. As much as it pained her heart to admit it, she was better off without him. The last thing she needed was to follow in her mother's footsteps and marry some untrustworthy man.

No. Dora Reynolds would remain true to herself, her family, and her friends. And no one else.

# Chapter Twenty

The minutes ticked by on Jacob's pocket watch. He'd set it on the desk as he worked his way through Peterson's shift. He'd only been scheduled to work through two in the afternoon, but at six, he'd received word that Peterson had taken ill and couldn't finish his shift. So Jake found himself behind the front desk again. It had been lively at first, with new passengers checking in and existing guests checking out to leave on the train that had just arrived.

But now, the evening rush had worn into a nighttime stupor. He should use the time and occupy his mind with his investigation, but all he could think about was Dora. Guilt gnawed away at the edges of his mind. He'd been so cold to her, and he was certain his suspicion shined through when he questioned her about the thief's motives. She'd shown no hint of sorrow or guilt. Still . . . who else could it be? No one else had the access. And while he wasn't entirely sure she had the motivation to steal the money, she'd said she was here to work for her family. And she'd all but said they depended upon her wages for survival. After all, who would send a beloved daughter hundreds of miles away to the frontier to work as a waitress if it wasn't absolutely necessary? Perhaps things had taken a turn for the worse at home, and Dora felt compelled to steal the money to aid the family she loved so much.

That explanation wasn't so horrible. In fact, Jacob felt himself sympathizing with her. He might even do the same for his own family if he were in such a situation. If there were no other options, and the wages he made working at whatever menial job he was qualified for weren't enough to keep his family in a decent home with enough to eat, he just might . . .

*That doesn't excuse it.* Jacob rubbed his hands across his face. His usually clean-shaven chin was beginning to grow a beard, something he would have never considered wearing back home in New York or during his time in Chicago. Despite the fashion, he'd much preferred a daily shave. But here . . . He could have laughed at himself. He hadn't shaved in days, he wore boots he would have sneered at two months ago, and he'd traded in his perfectly tailored jackets and trousers for those more befitting a desk clerk.

And he didn't seem to mind any of it one bit.

In fact, none of it had even crossed his mind until now. He'd been far too busy with his investigation and with—he had to admit—Dora. She certainly didn't mind his clothes or his unshaven face. She hadn't complained when he'd almost kissed her in the stables that evening . . .

"Pardon me, sir." A smartly dressed man stood before the front desk, unlit cigar in his hand. "I hear there are billiards tables in this hotel."

"There are, in the smoking parlor. Second door to the right." Jacob pointed to the other side of the front desk.

The man nodded, and just as he walked off, Jacob spotted her.

Dora, gliding across the lobby with a woman he didn't recognize. Neither of them wore the usual Gilbert Girls uniform dress. Instead, Dora wore a lively green frock that wasn't fancy in the least, but illuminated her skin and made her dark hair look even shinier than normal. It wasn't until she looked up at him that he realized he'd been staring. She said something to her companion, a slight blonde in blue and white, who then glanced up at him, unsmiling. Jacob nodded to her out of politeness, but looked back down at the desk as quickly as he could.

What had Dora said about him? His mind raced with the possibilities, none of them good. When he dared to glance up again, they were making their way up the stairs. Dora herself hadn't so much as acknowledged him, and that hurt more than anything she might have said to her friend.

Possessed with the urge to see her again—and make her see *him*—Jacob strode around the desk toward the stairs. He was halfway up when sense hit him. What would he do when he saw her? Was there anything he could say that might make up for how he'd acted earlier?

And should he? If she was the thief, he needed to keep his distance. And if she wasn't . . . Jacob curled his fingers around the banister. He needed to know.

He raced up the stairs, hoping the women were going to the parlor. If not, he'd be out of luck this evening, and he didn't know if he'd sleep at all tonight without a definitive answer. He entered the room, his eyes searching through the waitresses, maids, and other hotel employees until he found them.

Jacob strode through the parlor until he reached the corner in which they were sitting. There were no free chairs, so he stood awkwardly before them. Dora glanced up and then immediately looked back down at her lap. Her friend kept her eyes trained on Jacob.

"Good evening," he finally said, the rules of propriety, such as they were here, slowly returning to his head. Without Dora introducing him to her friend, he was left to do it himself. "I'm Jake James, desk clerk here at the hotel." He held out his hand, and the blonde woman laid hers in it.

"Mrs. Caroline Drexel, former Gilbert Girl," she said in a soft but pointed voice. He couldn't quite place her accent, but it was the cultured manner of speaking that came only from an upbringing similar to his own.

"Ah, of the general store?"

"Yes. I run the store with my husband."

Jacob had approximately nine hundred questions about how that had possibly come about, but he held his tongue. He was here to see Dora, to either put his doubts to rest or face the fact the woman he'd spent so much time with was actually stealing from his family's business. "Good evening, Miss Reynolds."

She glanced up at him again, her eyes shielded. The very look made him want to apologize until he was blue in the face. He'd hurt her.

Or had he? Was it a truthful look, or one she wished him to believe was truthful? Jacob's head spun. He needed to remain in control if he had any hope of discerning the truth.

"Good evening," she finally said, the words so cool she might as well have told him to have a terrible evening.

"I trust you're having a fine visit?"

"We are." She looked away from him to her friend.

"May we do something for you, Mr. James?" Mrs. Drexel finally asked. The words were friendly enough, but with an undertone that indicated they wished he'd leave.

Dora watched him now, her eyes blazing straight through to his soul. But her expression was anything but warm.

*It's for the best*, he reminded himself. He had a sole purpose here, and that wasn't falling for the wiles of a thief. *If she is the thief . . .*

"Mr. James?" Mrs. Drexel prompted.

"I'm sorry, I . . ." Why was he here? Did he think Dora would suddenly confess her crimes? "I simply wanted to make your acquaintance, given that I'm still new to the hotel."

Mrs. Drexel nodded, ever the bastion of politeness. He wondered what she really thought of him. Dora certainly made no secret of her feelings, with the way she'd seemed to turn as icy as Silver Creek was now behind the hotel. What did he expect, though, after pushing her away and indicating his suspicion?

"Then we'll bid you good evening, sir," Mrs. Drexel said.

"Good evening." He gave a polite bow and then turned on his heel. Only when he exited the door did he let down his guard. He leaned against the wall and ran a hand through his hair. Why did he think she'd confess or offer up some unquestionable alibi just because he followed her upstairs? And why did he worry so much about what she thought of him? She made a fine distraction, which may have been her intention all along.

He never should've let his affections get in the way of his work. He'd made a mess of everything, and now he might have to order the arrest of a woman he couldn't stop thinking about. If he could ever catch her, that is.

And yet . . . he couldn't shake the feeling that this was all wrong. No matter what the facts said, how could the time they'd spent together be all a lie? The way she'd looked at him right before he tried to kiss her in the stables . . . nothing had ever felt more real in his life. She had been genuinely upset that night when he'd comforted her. And what about the way she'd tried to keep him at a distance when he was first getting to know her? He'd thought she was a refreshing change from the practiced flirts he'd known in Chicago and New York. But was it something else?

What was real? And what was made up?

When he returned downstairs, his thoughts still running circles in his mind, Mr. Thomason, the depot clerk, waited at the front desk. Who knew how long the man had been standing there, since Jacob had abandoned his post to chase after a woman.

"I was told you'd be here tonight," he said when Jacob slid behind the desk. "I have a telegram for you. Thought I'd bring it over before closing up for the night."

Jacob thanked him and handed him a coin for his trouble. Once the clerk had left and Jacob had taken stock of those who remained in the lobby, he unfolded the paper and flattened it on the desk. Drawing the lamp closer, he read:

*JG had change of heart. Feels you to be more useful here. Return on next train. JG, Jr.*

Jacob crumpled the telegram in his fist. His father couldn't even be bothered to send the message himself, making his brother be the bearer of bad news. He itched to chase Thomason down with an insistent message that he had five more days. But all that might do was make his father angrier.

He stared out over the lobby. There was nothing to do but return to Denver and plead his case.

# Chapter Twenty-one

Dora was quiet when Jake left the parlor. Her emotions felt as if they were fighting each other, and she wasn't sure how she should feel, much less how she actually felt. Why had he come upstairs? Had he planned to interrogate her again and only stopped when he saw she was with Caroline? She'd found nothing in her and Millie's room that would serve as proof Millie was the thief, so she couldn't have even used that to defend herself from his accusations.

Caroline laid a hand on her arm. "Are you all right?"

"I don't know." Dora squeezed her eyes shut. She'd cried enough over this man. He didn't deserve any more of her tears. "I wish my mother were here." Her mother would know the right words to say to soothe Dora's battered soul. She'd never ached for her mother's embrace the way she did now.

Caroline took her hand and stood, gently pulling Dora up. "Come, let's go somewhere more private."

Dora followed her friend numbly. She hadn't seen as much of Caroline since she'd married and gone to live with her husband at the new general store. But Caroline was an excellent listener who always had good advice, and Dora was thankful she had happened to stop by the hotel for a visit.

Caroline led her down the hall to Penny's room. Penny answered right away and swept Caroline up in a hug. "Oh! I'm so glad you're here. I need your help. Now, for the wedding—" She stopped the moment she saw Dora.

Dora figured she must look a fright, because Penny pulled her into a hug too. When Penny let her go, she kept hold of her arms as she studied Dora's face. "It's that man, isn't it?"

Dora pushed her lips together, trying to keep her emotions from taking over yet again. She nodded quickly, not trusting herself to speak.

"He followed us upstairs to the lobby, for what seemed to be no apparent reason," Caroline told Penny.

But Penny kept her eyes on Dora. "You do have feelings for him, don't you?"

Dora nodded again, more slowly this time. She should've trusted her friends from the beginning. Especially Penny. She, Caroline, and Emma—whom they all looked forward to seeing as soon as she made her way back to the valley with her husband—only had each other for months when they first arrived in Crest Stone. Dora trusted these women like her own family.

But not enough to tell them who she really was. That truth ate away at her conscience, more so now than ever.

"Oh, my poor dear." Penny drew her into a hug again before letting her go to sit on the bed. Caroline took the chair at the desk, while Dora sunk onto the mattress next to Penny. "What did he do?"

She'd only briefly told Caroline that Jake had played with her affections, giving her attention until he'd seen she had developed feelings for him before pushing her away. It was the truth, and she told Penny as much now, even if it wasn't the entire truth. "It's for the best," she finished.

Caroline wrapped her fingers tightly around the reticule she carried. "What do you mean?"

"If you mean because it's forbidden, well . . ." Penny gave a knowing glance at Caroline.

Dora knew exactly what they were referring to. Each of her friends had found love, even though it was against the rules of being a Gilbert Girl. "It's not that. Well, yes, it is, but only to an extent." If she kept talking, perhaps she could keep her head about her instead of dissolving into a teary mess again. She tucked a strand of hair behind her ear as her friends waited patiently for her explanation. How could she share how heart-rending it was to know he suspected her of thievery, without giving away his true purpose here or her involvement in the investigation? Even though he'd betrayed her affections, she felt it best to keep the investigation a secret, for the good of the hotel. And perhaps also for Jake's safety. If word got out to the thief, Jake might be in danger.

Instead, she concentrated on the strange feeling she'd had during their conversation outside, that he hadn't been entirely honest with her either. "I had the oddest feeling the last time we spoke. It was as if . . ." It was hard to put into words. "As if he knows more about certain ways of life than he should."

At Penny and Caroline's quizzical expressions, she tried to explain it better. "He grew up in Chicago, and his father was a policeman. Yet, his good friends were quite well-to-do, and he speaks of impoverished people as if they have all sorts of options. While I imagine his family wasn't poor, I doubt they were wealthy either. It doesn't fit together."

"Do you think he's lying?" Penny asked.

Dora lifted her eyes to Penny's window, the blinding white world outside offering no answers. She tried to imagine what it might be like to live as a policeman's son in Chicago, but it was so far removed from her own experience, she didn't know where to begin. "I don't know. I don't know enough about that life to be certain. It simply strikes me as strange." She turned to look back at her friends, both of whom had grown up in cities, albeit in entirely different circumstances. "Do boys from working-class families normally spend time with the children of wealthy families?"

Both Caroline and Penny shook their heads.

"My brother befriended the son of a fruit seller when we were children. It was allowed until he was about twelve, and then Father put an end to it," Caroline said.

"My friends were all of the same station," Penny added. She wrinkled her brow. "And when Mama and I fell on difficult times, we accepted some help from the church, but they certainly didn't have enough to give everyone all they needed when they needed it. It was helpful, but it was hardly the answer to improving our situation. That only came with me leaving to work here."

Dora twisted her hands together in her lap. Penny and Caroline had confirmed her suspicions. "I fear that Jake isn't who he says he is."

"Then who is he?" Caroline asked.

"Perhaps he's a European prince in disguise," Penny said, her eyes wide. "Come to live among the common folk."

"He has no accent," Caroline said. "Your imagination has taken off with you."

"Or maybe he's the son of a disgraced politician," Penny said, ignoring Caroline. "Forced to make a life for himself after the downfall of his family. That's quite tragic, don't you think?"

She was so earnest that Dora couldn't help but laugh just a little. It felt good, sitting here with her friends, even though her life had gone topsy-turvy.

But there was something about what Penny had said that actually made sense. Given the reason Jake had said he was here, perhaps he was forced to pretend to be someone he was not. If that was the case, though, why hadn't he told her? The thought riled up her anger all over again, even as a tiny voice reminded her she'd done the exact same thing to him.

"Dora," Caroline said, rising from her chair and resettling herself on Adelaide's bed across from Penny's. "Why don't you simply ask him?"

The very idea curled up like a ball in Dora's stomach, weighing her down. "I couldn't."

"Why not?" Penny asked. "You deserve to know the truth."

Did she? Especially if she was equally culpable? She couldn't reciprocate, after all. Not only would he most certainly suspect her of stealing the money after that, he might tell Mrs. Ruby and the McFarlands, and then she'd be cast out of her job here. And what if his opinion of her changed even more than it seemingly already had?

Dora covered her face with her hands. It was all too much. And yet if they'd gone on with . . . whatever it was they had together, when would she have told him the truth? Never?

The horrible guilt that constantly sat inside—the one that reminded her now and then that she was a terrible person for denying her own family—came raging up like fire in the dry season. Dora bit down on her lip to keep from crying.

"Dora?" Penny wrapped an arm around her. "Are you all right?"

Dora shook her head, her face still in her hands.

"Can you tell us what's wrong?" Caroline asked. She was on the floor now, her hand resting on Dora's knee.

Dora took a great, gulping breath, pulling her hands away. She forced herself to continue breathing as normally as possible. "I can't ask him."

Caroline looked at Penny, who finally asked, "Why not?"

"I simply can't. Because if he knew . . ." She couldn't finish the sentence. The fear of losing her friends was too great. Penny and Caroline couldn't help who they were. They'd likely been raised to think ill of her people. And while it would feel marvelous to finally confess her true identity, she couldn't bear the thought of losing their friendship. And if she couldn't tell them, how could she possibly tell Jake?

"Knew what?" Caroline prodded.

But Dora straightened her back and forced herself to give Caroline a slight smile. "Nothing. Please, I don't wish to talk about Jake any longer. I'd much rather hear about Penny's wedding."

"All right . . ." Penny said uncertainly as she exchanged glances with Caroline again.

And as Penny spoke, Dora half listened. She was realizing the only cure for keeping Jake from her mind and retaining her work at the hotel was to locate the thief. She could conduct her own investigation, only involving him in the most cursory way. If she put all her effort into that, instead of letting her mind go round and round about Jake, she might just be able to save the hotel.

She just wasn't certain if she could save her heart.

# Chapter Twenty-two

The mountains rose sharply to the west outside Jake's window, arching toward the sky and glittering in the late afternoon sun under a pristine coat of snow. They were likely an hour or so outside of Denver, and his mind hadn't stopped working since he'd left Crest Stone the evening before. Even his sleep in a hotel in Cañon City last night had been punctuated by dreams of Dora, facing his father, and returning home to live with his mother in New York. It was a bleak future, and not one he relished beginning any time soon.

The train rocked and swayed beneath him as it made its way north. He'd hoped it would lull him into sleep this morning, but he hadn't been so lucky. It was impossible for his body to rest when his mind wouldn't.

He focused on the unchanging peaks out the window, wondering what Dora was doing at this moment. Perhaps she was serving lunch to hotel guests. It was long past noon, so the train to Santa Fe would have already left the depot in Crest Stone. Had she noticed he was gone?

He'd only seen her from a distance yesterday before he left. She'd glanced his way a couple of times but didn't acknowledge him. Her stony looks felt like they'd turned his own heart into rock. He kept telling himself it was inevitable, especially now that the investigation was over and he was leaving. What would he have done? Brought her with him into a life that was now filled with uncertainty?

Besides, she might be the thief.

No, he was better off leaving her behind and figuring out how to begin his life anew.

"Pardon me, could I trouble you for a match?" The man seated across the aisle now stood next to Jacob. He held an unlit cigar in his hand.

Jacob felt around his pockets until he found one and handed it to the man.

"My thanks," he said, as soon as he'd lit the cigar. He puffed on the end of it a few times before sitting down again. "Fine morning for a ride up the rails, isn't it?"

"It is," Jacob agreed. He didn't feel much like conversing, but perhaps this was what he needed to stop thinking about Dora. "What's your business in Denver?"

The man grinned at him around the cigar. "I'm fetching my wife. She's not my wife yet, but we'll be married later today or tomorrow. And then returning home with her."

"Congratulations," Jacob said, wishing he'd never asked. But now curiosity had the best of him, and he asked, "Have you been engaged long?"

The man laughed this time, a hearty chuckle loud enough for every person in their car to hear. "Oh, no. I ordered her, you see."

"Ordered her?"

"By mail. I wrote away to an agency back East that finds suitable women to marry men here in the Territory. And elsewhere, I suppose."

Jacob nodded, trying not to show his surprise that anyone would do such a thing. He'd heard of such services, but had never met anyone who'd used one. The possibilities for something to go wrong seemed great, and yet it made some amount of sense, particularly in a place like the Colorado Territory, where women were few and far between. He wondered what Dora would think of it.

The man was looking him up and down now. "I don't know what sort of business you're in, but if you're in need of a wife, you should order one too."

"I'm in the hotel business, and I'm not in need of a wife," Jacob said immediately.

"Ah, got someone you're sweet on already," the man said knowingly. "Is she here or back East?"

"Here," Jacob said before realizing the word was out of his mouth. "I mean, there's no woman." He was likely no longer in the hotel business either, but he didn't particularly feel like sharing that bit of information with a stranger.

With that the man sat back, studying Jacob thoroughly now. Thankfully, he was too polite to ask more questions. "I'll tell you, I've spent years in the mining business. Started it myself, from a lucky find outside Cripple Creek. Bane of my father's existence. He'd hoped I'd fail and return to Charleston, my tail between my legs. Instead, I've got a business that rivals his in profit now. But I digress. I had a girl for a while in Denver, but she grew tired of seeing me only once every few months. And I was too preoccupied with my mines to realize that. She married another man, and I thought it didn't bother me. Until about a month ago, when I sat down to a cold, stale dinner, all alone. Then it hit me how stupid I'd been." He laughed before taking another puff of his cigar. "Don't be like me. If there is a girl, don't let her get away. And if there isn't, well, order yourself one."

Jacob didn't know what to say to all of that. The man unfolded a newspaper and began reading, seemingly finished with conversation, and Jacob turned back to the window.

Was he being foolish, like the man said? Dora met new men every day, and although she wasn't allowed to be courted, what was to stop one of them from capturing her heart anyway? The very thought made his fists clench.

But he couldn't marry a thief, especially one who stole from his family's own company. *If* he wanted to marry her, that is. And if he did, how would he support her? His father would probably still let him work in the office. Chief File Boy and Errand Runner. He couldn't continue like that. He already knew he'd need to strike out on his own, somehow. And how could he do that with a wife in tow? Not to mention, Dora was hardly of his same station. That didn't bother him at all, but what would his father think? He might not care; he was rather accepting of such things—at least when they were done outside of his own family. But why did Jacob care what his father thought, especially now that he was likely never going to move up in the company?

He glanced across the way at the man with the cigar. Jacob pegged him to be only about ten years his senior. He'd been so intent on his new business that he'd let the woman he loved slip through his fingers. Jacob rubbed his hand across his face, and tried—in vain—not to imagine himself in the same position. And there was something else . . . Not in what the man had said, but something entirely different that had been bothering him for a few days now.

It wasn't in what his father might think, or in Jacob's plans for the future. It had nothing to do with his family at all. It was Dora, that much he could figure out. But what?

He let his mind wander as the train slowed just outside of Denver. And as the whistle blew, he grabbed hold of the bothersome thought.

*Dora was hardly of his same station.* Yes, but he knew that. He'd pretended to be a working-class policeman's son in Crest Stone. And she was . . . what, exactly? She'd never told him. She spoke little of Chicago, and now that he traced back through their conversations, it became clear she had only agreed with him about favorite places in the city or certain landmarks. She'd never once mentioned one herself. Except the lake, but everyone knew the city was on the lake.

She wasn't from Chicago.

The realization was like a twig catching fire. If she wasn't from Chicago, then why would she pretend to be? It fit in perfectly with his suspicion that she was the thief, except it could also mean something else entirely. It was obvious now that she was keeping some kind of secret. But whether it was that she was stealing money from the hotel, or something else entirely that made him *think* she was the thief because that was the closest and easiest answer . . . that was unclear.

He didn't know what Dora's secret was, but he needed to find out. He had to talk to her and ask her directly for the truth. And, he admitted to himself, he needed to tell her the truth about himself too. He couldn't expect her to be honest with him if he didn't afford her the same courtesy.

But first, he had to face his father.

# Chapter Twenty-three

Dora hadn't seen Jake at the front desk for days now. She hadn't wanted to ask anyone where he was for fear of giving away the fact that she'd spent so much time with him. But the not knowing was constantly worrying her. Was he ill? Had he given up the investigation and abandoned his position? Had he—she didn't want to think this, but had to acknowledge the possibility—returned to Chicago?

There had been no word of more money going missing in the past few days, and for that, Dora was thankful. She only wished she knew what had happened to Jake.

After finishing the dinner service one evening, she felt as if she couldn't take the not knowing any longer. Her gaze was drawn, as usual, toward the front desk as she passed it with Penny and Adelaide.

Penny squeezed her arm. "Why don't you go ask Mr. Peterson?"

Dora glanced back at her friend, who smiled in return.

"At least then you'll know," Penny added. Adelaide wrinkled her brow, looking back and forth between them.

Dora drew a deep breath and took a step toward the desk—then stopped. What would Mr. Peterson think of her for asking about Jake? Which was worse—not knowing or having Mr. Peterson think ill of her? She straightened and pushed her shoulders back. She needed to know.

"Good evening, Mr. Peterson," she said when she reached the desk. Thankfully, it was late, and no hotel guests were nearby. She wrapped her hands around the edge of the desk to keep them from shaking.

He gave her a tired but friendly smile. "Good evening, Miss Reynolds. What can I do for you?"

Dora swallowed, then forced herself to speak. "I'm hoping you might know what has become of Mr. James. I—well . . . We, I mean, the girls and I—" She gestured at Penny and Adelaide. "We've worried he's fallen ill and wondered if he might need anything." The last words flew out of her mouth in a rush, and Dora held on to the edge of the desk even tighter.

Mr. Peterson gave her a sad smile. "I'm sorry to tell you Mr. James has left his position here at the hotel. I believe he may have returned home. He said he had a family affair to tend to."

"Oh." Dora forced herself to nod and thank the man before walking back to her friends. It felt as if she'd been drained of everything that gave her life, and all she was now was a walking shadow.

Penny took her arm and guided her to the stairs, Adelaide hurrying behind them. Not until they'd reached the top of the stairs, far from prying eyes, did she speak. "It isn't good news, I take it? Are you all right?"

Dora kept all her attention on Penny's words and Penny's hand around her arm. If she let her mind wander—if she thought about the meaning behind the words Mr. Peterson had spoken to her—she would fall apart. "I am fine," she said carefully, although she wasn't entirely certain she was. "Mr. James has returned to Chicago to tend to his family."

They'd reached Dora's room, and Penny stopped. "Why don't you come sit with me and Adelaide for a while?"

"I'm fine, I promise you." Dora even gave Penny a little smile. "All I need right now is a good night of sleep."

Penny narrowed her eyes, and for a moment, Dora feared Penny could see the thoughts she was hiding. "All right," Penny finally said. "But if you need anything at all, we're just down the hallway."

Adelaide nodded. Even though Dora hadn't told her everything she'd shared with Penny and Caroline, Adelaide clearly suspected Dora had feelings for Jake.

Dora said good night to her friends, and then faced her door. Millie was likely inside, either getting ready to sleep or possibly already asleep. Dora needed to keep her feelings about Jake's departure to herself, at least until she discovered whether Millie was the thief.

She turned the knob and stepped inside. A lamp burned brightly on the desk, where Millie sat in her nightclothes, penning what Dora guessed to be a letter. Shadows cast from the lamp's light danced around the small but cozy room, and all Dora could think at that very moment was how much she loved

living in this room at this hotel. She'd never had a home without her family before, and had feared she'd never be comfortable in a place without them. But
even though she missed her mother and everyone else, she felt at home here.

A great sob rose in her chest as she thought about the hotel possibly closing.
It couldn't happen. It *wouldn't*. Even if Jake had given up, Dora would not. She
forced down the overwhelming urge to throw herself onto the bed and cry, and
instead, fixed her gaze on Millie.

"How was the dinner service?" Millie asked as she dipped her pen into a
bottle of ink.

"It went well," Dora replied. She walked toward Millie and took a seat at
the foot of her bed, which abutted the desk. She smoothed her skirts and tried
to summon the courage she knew she'd need for what she was about to say next.

"Did Adelaide finally manage to clear her tables in a decent amount of
time?" Millie asked. Adelaide had taken to being a Gilbert Girl quickly, but she
adored talking with her guests more than anything else and had immediately
become the one waitress at dinner who still had tables filled with guests after
nine o'clock, when every other girl had already seen her guests out and cleared
her tables.

"Not yet," Dora said. "But she's at least finally understood that the train passengers can't linger." Dora clasped her hands in her lap. "Millie? May I ask you
a question?"

Millie paused in her writing and laid her pen down. "Of course you may."
She looked Dora up and down, her red curls escaping the braid she'd attempted
to tame them into for the night. "Is something wrong?"

So much was wrong that Dora wanted nothing more than to throw herself
into her friend's arms and tell her everything. But she couldn't, at least not until
she'd found out the truth. She drew in a deep breath, and said, "I need to know
if you are the one who has been stealing from the hotel."

Millie's mouth fell open, but before she could speak, Dora rushed to say
more. "If you are, I promise not to say anything to Mr. McFarland or Mrs. Ruby
if you return the money, even if that takes time. I only need to know the truth."

Millie stood, her face as hard as the mountains that stood outside their window. She closed the ink bottle and didn't look at Dora.

"Millie?" Dora pressed, desperation leaking into her voice. "Please, just tell me the truth. The hotel won't be able to operate much longer if the thefts continue."

"I thought you were my friend." Millie finally looked at Dora, her hands on the back of the desk chair.

"I am. I will still be your friend, even if—"

"Even if I'm a thief? How could you think such a thing? What about me ever gave you the idea I might be stealing from the hotel?" Millie burst out.

Dora wanted to curl in on herself. What had she expected Millie to do? Confess and ask for forgiveness? "You're the only one . . ." She trailed off, not necessarily wanting Millie to know the true reason she'd been downstairs so late at night. "Both of those nights I ran into you downstairs were nights that money was stolen."

"So you immediately assumed I'm the culprit?" Millie had her hands on her hips now. "What about you? How should I know *you* aren't the one stealing from the Crest Stone?"

Dora squeezed her eyes shut. That was exactly what she feared Jake had thought, too. Emotions swirled up inside her, threatening to take over. *No.* She forced her feelings for Jake back down. Keeping the hotel open was the most important thing right now. "I am not."

Millie threw up her hands. "Neither am I!"

"How come you stopped by the office door that night?" Dora pressed. "Had you lost *that* key?"

"Of course not! I told you I'd lost the key to our room when I'd met up with Mr. Graham, which was foolish of me after all. He hasn't so much as glanced my way since then." Millie's lower lip trembled, and for a moment, Dora thought she might burst into tears. "I am terrible at choosing the right men. I should know that about myself by now. That's why I never said anything to you or the others."

Dora opened her mouth to try to comfort Millie, but her friend seemed to push her feelings aside and press on. "I'd stopped to search for my key in the hallway that night. That's all. What else do I need to say to convince you?"

Dora looked down at her hands. She'd been wrong. She knew this as much as she knew her own heart. She'd found nothing in Millie's things that had proven she'd taken the money, after all. "I'm so sorry. It's only that you were the only suspect we had, and I got carried away with hoping I'd be able to put an end to all of this. I didn't want it to be you, I promise." She looked up at Millie now, her friend's arms still crossed. "I'm grateful it isn't you. I . . . I don't know how I can make it up to you." Guilt seeped through her words. What sort of friend suspected one of being a thief, after all? She'd likely ruined her friendship with Millie forever. "I'll ask Mrs. Ruby if I can move in with Sarah, since she has an extra bed."

Millie shook her head with an exasperated sigh. "Don't be ridiculous. I'm still angry with you, but there's no need for you to move elsewhere."

Dora chewed on her lip. She dared not hope Millie might eventually forgive her.

"What did you mean by 'we'?"

Dora's heart sunk. She hadn't even noticed she'd slipped and included Jake in her explanation. "I didn't mean anything by it."

Millie's expression almost looked like Penny's as she tilted her head and studied Dora. "Yes, you did. Did you mean your gentleman friend? Mr. James?"

Dora squeezed her eyes shut. She didn't want to think about Jake. Not right now.

"You did." Millie's voice had lost some of its cold edge. "You weren't simply skulking about the hallways so late only to meet up with him, were you?"

Dora shook her head, still not daring to open her eyes for fear of losing every ounce of control she was desperately clinging to.

"You were trying to catch the thief." Millie paused. "I haven't seen Mr. James lately. Has he been ill?"

And with that, Dora couldn't hold back the emotions pressing on her from every side. They burst forth like the spring melt thawed all at once. Tears streamed down her face and great, wracking sobs shook her body. She wrapped her arms around herself, wishing with everything she had that she was at home with her mother.

Arms wrapped around her, and a hand pressed her head to a shoulder. Millie.

Dora clung to her friend, the one she didn't deserve. Not after she'd accused her of stealing.

"Shh." Millie held her until her sobs eased. And then Dora told her everything, unburdening herself of her feelings for Jake, their investigation and failure to catch the thief, the way Jake had seemed to suspect Dora, his coldness toward her, her suspicion that he might not be who he said he was, and now his disappearance without a word.

"He's a coward," Millie said when Dora finished. "You can't trust a man with a secret. I should know."

She was right, to an extent. After all, Millie's first beau when she'd come to Crest Stone had turned out to be a conniving, selfish man who'd set the hotel on fire. But Jake was no Mr. Turner. Dora knew that with all her heart.

"I wish you'd had the opportunity to confront him and ask him for the truth," Millie said, her arm still around Dora's shoulders.

"I couldn't have," Dora said, the old fear tingling up her spine. Her secret had always felt as if she was standing on the precipice between this world and the next, the slightest wind able to blow her into a future of nothing.

"You could. You're braver than you think you are."

"It isn't that . . ." Dora took a shuddering breath. She needed to tell someone. Someone she could trust. If she could at least completely unburden herself to one person, perhaps she wouldn't feel the need to hide all the time. She wiped her eyes and twisted to look at her friend. "Millie, tell me, what do you think of the Indians?"

Millie furrowed her brow, seemingly caught off-guard at Dora's change of subject. "I . . . Well, I suppose I don't think anything about them. I've never met one. I imagine I'd make up my mind once I did."

That was all Dora needed. "You have." She clenched the bedcovers between her fingers. "I'm of the Ute tribe. My mother is Muache. My father, I've heard, was a white man."

Millie blinked at her.

And Dora feared she'd made the greatest mistake of her entire life.

# Chapter Twenty-four

Jacob stood in front of his father, his brother taking up his usual position in the chair to the right. The old man had been railing at him for twenty minutes straight, accusing him of wasting the company's time and letting money slip through his fingers. Jacob had expected no less. He'd failed in his mission, after all.

But as the one-sided conversation droned on and on, Jacob found himself caring less and less. Certainly, he still worried that the thief was at large and the hotel was in danger of closing. But as his father accused him of still being a careless college boy, he came to understand a truth that had been slowly awakening inside himself ever since he'd disembarked at the depot.

He was no entitled young man in search of only the next good time. Not anymore.

It no longer mattered what his father or his brother or anyone else thought he was, because Jacob himself *knew* exactly who he was. He had grown measurably since coming to Denver, and even more since spending that short time in Crest Stone. He was more than capable of finding his own way, somehow. And while he regretted he hadn't been able to uncover the thief, he'd made his best effort. And he'd done that with Dora by his side.

He'd been wrong, thinking she was a distraction. She'd helped him, and he'd cast her aside because he'd made an assumption that he was growing increasingly certain was untrue.

He needed to be somewhere else, and that somewhere was not in his father's office in Denver.

"We cannot coddle you for the rest of your life," Father was saying, his face as red as a holly berry. "How do you expect to survive once I'm gone? How do you ever expect to support a family of your own?" He paused and frowned. "Are you listening to me, Jacob?"

Jacob stared at the door. "I need to return."

"Return? You'll return to New York on the next train. I—"

"No." Jacob turned now to face Father. Out of the corner of his eye, he saw his brother sit up just a little straighter in his chair. Neither of them had ever told Father no.

The man placed a hand on his desk and blinked, as if he wasn't entirely certain he'd heard Jacob correctly. But before he could speak, Jacob plowed on.

"You weren't there. You didn't see how much effort I put into this assignment. Yes, I failed, but it wasn't for lack of trying." He shook his head. It was useless defending himself, and after all, what did it matter now? "I no longer care for a place in this company. I don't know what I'll do, and perhaps I'll fail again. But I'll find my own way. And that starts with returning to Crest Stone. I have some unfinished business I need to take care of there."

And with that, he strode to the door. But before he left, he turned quickly back to face his stunned father and brother. "Thank you for the opportunity to be a part of this business. I wish you success."

He thought he saw James smile just a bit before he made his way out the door and toward the depot. His future was uncertain, but only one thing mattered right now.

Dora.

# Chapter Twenty-five

D ora felt as if she were one of the Sangre de Cristo peaks, waking up in the spring to find the snow melting away. Ever since telling Millie about her family and her true identity, she'd felt lighter and somehow less burdened, even though she still kept her secret from everyone else.

Jake was gone. It pinched at her heart that he'd left so suddenly and without a word to her. She wished she could do everything all over again. If she had a second chance, she'd confess to him the way she had to Millie. Whether or not he accepted her, she doubted he would have told the McFarlands or Mrs. Ruby. Perhaps then she'd have asked him for the same, and he'd have told her whatever secret he was hiding. Because it was clear as the icicles that hung from the hotel roof that he'd also kept something from her. And then, if they'd needed to part, at least they could have done so with clear consciences.

Dora tried not to dwell too much on the regret that it hadn't ended in that way. She couldn't go back and fix it; she needed to accept that it was over and he would not be returning. Her priority was her work—and finding the thief. She refused to give up on the hotel.

Dora mulled over ideas as she worked, relaying the best ones to Millie. But so far, nothing they had come up with had been very good. She set down the stack of dirty linens she carried, piling them into a basket for the hotel maids to wash, then brushed back a strand of hair with the back of her arm before returning to the dining room.

A few guests still sat at tables, finishing dinner or having cake and coffee. It was going on eight thirty, and all of Dora's tables had emptied.

"Dora!" Mrs. Ruby bustled up to her from one of the nearby serving stations. "Since your tables are cleared, I'm hoping you can do me a favor."

"Of course. What do you need?" Dora said, even though she wished to be dismissed instead. It had been a long, hard day, and all she cared to do right now was tumble into her bed for a good night's sleep.

"Edie is upstairs abed with fever. Could you take a small tray to Mrs. McFarland with coffee and a slice of cake?"

Dora nodded. It was Edie's usual nightly chore, as Mrs. McFarland's recipes were often used for dessert in the dining room and she liked to ensure they'd turned out well.

Dora returned to the kitchen for a tray and a slice of cake, then stopped at a station on her way back through the dining room for hot coffee and milk in a delicate china cup. She carried the tray carefully through the lobby, forcing herself not to glance at the front desk. It had become a bad habit, looking to see if Jake had miraculously reappeared. It was high time she faced reality and stopped wishing for things that would not happen. And she almost succeeded.

She had just reached the stairs when her head seemed to turn of its own accord. Of course, he wasn't there. Dora sighed, partly from disappointment and partly from irritation with herself. She'd do better next time and not look at all.

She passed a couple of the hotel maids and a few guests returning to their rooms as she walked down the hall to the hotel office. She knocked lightly on the door, hoping she wasn't disturbing the McFarlands' work. "It's Dora, with your cake and coffee."

"One moment, please," Mrs. McFarland's voice said through the closed door.

Dora shifted the weight of the tray in her hands, eager to finish this chore and get to her room for the night.

The door's lock clicked from the other side, and then it opened to Mrs. McFarland, whose face was drawn and whose strawberry-blonde hair looked lank instead if its usual vibrant color.

"Pardon me, Mrs. McFarland, but are you well?" Dora stepped inside.

"Oh, yes. I am. It's simply all this mess with the missing money. Michael insists I keep the door locked when I'm in here alone. I believe he's afraid the thief might force his way in to get to the safe. It's a lot to handle." She drew her hands across her face and then shook her head. "I'm sorry, Dora. I don't mean to worry you about it. Where is Edie this evening?"

"I'm afraid she's fallen ill."

"Well, I'm sorry to hear that. She's a delightful girl, if a bit on the skittish side. Thank you for bringing me the cake. That's one of Michael's favorite recipes. You can set it down on my desk." She pointed to the light wood desk to the right of the door, the one that was delicately carved and covered with stacks of paper . . . and money.

Dora swallowed hard as she took in how much was likely sitting on the desk. It had to be hundreds of dollars, the bills stacked and some neatly bound in various denominations.

"I fear you've caught me in the middle of settling our accounts. It's always something in a place like this." She glanced at the stacks of money and paper, worry creasing lines on her face.

"Do you—" Dora paused and took a breath, her heart thumping hard inside her chest as a new idea began to form in her head. "Do you settle accounts every night?" The question felt intrusive the second it was out of her mouth, so she added, "It seems like a lot of work."

Mrs. McFarland smiled. "Oh, it is. And no, thankfully. I'd like to make payments only once a week, but it's often more frequent that that. There's always someone to be paid for supplies, food, work. I don't mind it—I enjoy keeping the books, after all . . ." She trailed off before shaking her head as if to clear her thoughts. "Thank you for the dessert, dear. It's getting late. I do hope Mrs. Ruby is done with you for the evening." She held the door open for Dora.

"Oh, I imagine she is," Dora said, even though her mind was elsewhere. She cast a quick glance around the room before stepping toward the door. All else looked to be in place, Mr. McFarland's desk neat and tidy, the fire crackling in the fireplace, and the safe . . . The safe was wide open.

Dora rushed to the door and bade Mrs. McFarland good night. The lock clicked behind her, but Dora barely heard it. She walked as quickly as possible back to the dining room, her mind racing faster than her legs.

They'd been wrong. The money hadn't been stolen when everyone was asleep.

It had been stolen right under Mrs. McFarland's watch.

# Chapter Twenty-six

J acob emerged from the train car into the bright winter sun. He blinked and shielded his eyes in the noon sun as he stood on the small platform. Other passengers disembarked around him, some moving toward the carriages waiting to drive them up the hill to the hotel and restaurant, and others walking that same direction on foot through the snow.

He had neither the time nor the patience for a carriage, especially for such a short distance. A small case clutched in his hand, he made his way up the hill, quickly passing most of the other passengers who moved at a more leisurely pace.

Once inside the hotel, he paused. He hadn't expected this strange feeling—this feeling of returning *home*—at all. But there it was, reaching through him like a long-forgotten memory. The imposing and yet somehow comfortable hotel lobby seemed the place he was meant to be. He tried to clear his head as a few other passengers entered behind him and moved toward the dining room and the lunch counter for the noon meal.

Jacob hadn't planned much beyond simply returning to Crest Stone. And while he'd certainly run every scenario of his reunion with Dora through his head multiple times, he hadn't thought through where he would find her. So, he followed the other passengers, figuring chances were good that she was serving lunch.

Inside the dining room, he paused to scan the room for her. Girls in gray dresses and white aprons scurried here and there, and it took a moment before he laid eyes on Dora at the far end of the room. He quickly made his way toward her section of tables and found an open one near the wall. He sat and waited.

But his first visitor was not Dora. Instead, a man about his own age had come bustling across the room, half out of breath, and stood before the table

"Pardon me, sir," he said, adjusting a vest that seemed to enjoy riding up his round stomach. "But would you mind terribly if I joined you for this meal?"

Jacob glanced across the room. Sure enough, all the tables had filled. He nodded at the man, even as he groaned inwardly. How could he speak with Dora when he had an audience?

"I thank you. The name's Aaron Cardwell." The man thrust a hand across the table.

Jacob shook the man's cold yet sweaty hand, then quietly wiped his own hand along the side of his pants. "Jake James," he said, keeping up the ruse. Dora would be the first to know who he really was, not this nervous creature of a man.

"Pleasure," Mr. Cardwell said as he picked up the menu that lay on the table in front of him.

Jacob hadn't even looked at the thing when Dora glided up to them.

"Good afternoon, gentlemen," she said in her soft voice. "I'm Miss Reynolds. May I—" Her voice faltered as her eyes landed on Jacob.

He gave her an unrestrained smile. One quickly flitted across her face, only to disappear into concern. He supposed it should have been an expected reaction. He had, after all, taken off to Denver without so much as a word.

"Water is fine with me," Jacob said, answering her unasked question. He didn't even hear what his tablemate ordered. He was too focused on taking in every aspect of Dora's beautiful face and trying to read her reaction to him. When she turned back to him, he clutched the edges of his chair lest he leap up and take her into his arms.

"Mr. James?" she asked, likely not for the first time.

"I apologize," he said, fumbling for his menu. The words swam before his eyes. "I'll take any dish you might recommend."

He could see her swallow as she lifted her pad of paper to write. "The beef, then. Our chef does wonders with beef."

"Well, that sounds good to me too," the man across from Jacob said.

Dora nodded. "I'll have those out to you soon so you'll have plenty of time to eat before reboarding your train."

"I'm staying," Jacob said immediately.

Her eyes lifted from the paper to him. "Are you certain?"

Her words pierced his heart. "Yes. Absolutely certain."

"All right." She gave them both a small smile. "I'll return soon."

Cardwell's eyes followed her as she walked to the kitchen door. "She's awfully pretty."

Jacob narrowed his eyes at the man, whose carefully greased hair was now falling across his forehead. "The waitresses at this hotel hold the finest reputations." His words held an edge he hadn't meant to use, but he figured it was better than forcing this man to take his eyes off Dora.

"Oh, I didn't mean to imply . . . I only . . ." Cardwell pulled a lace-edged handkerchief from his pocket and wiped his brow even though the room was a comfortable temperature. "You seem to know her?"

"I've been here before," Jacob said shortly.

Cardwell stumbled out some more words, which Jacob didn't hear. Dora had reemerged from the kitchen and was now taking more orders. She moved through the room like a swan on water. He itched to speak with her alone. He had so much to say, to ask, that he didn't even know where he'd start.

When she brought them their plates of food, he tried to catch her eye. She looked at him briefly but gave no hint to what she might be thinking.

Jacob ate his food as quickly as possible, even though his appetite had disappeared entirely. Cardwell nattered on about a sales position he hoped to take in Santa Fe. When Dora came to collect their plates and payment, Jacob handed her some bills and a small note he'd managed to write while Cardwell talked at length about everything from medicinal sales to sales of ladies' hats. Jacob figured the man had sold just about everything that could possibly be sold west of the Mississippi. He gathered his hat and case, bid the man farewell, and went to await Dora's arrival.

If she chose to see him, that is.

# Chapter Twenty-seven

Dora couldn't decide if she felt sick or excited. Her stomach turned as if she'd caught some winter illness and yet her heart fluttered, about to take wing right out of her body.

"Go now," Millie whispered to her. "I'll clear your tables and take care of any new customers who come in." She gave Dora a little push on the shoulder as she took her tray of dirty glassware.

Dora nodded her thanks. She pinched her cheeks and smoothed down her hair before leaving the dining room. Thankfully, Mrs. Ruby was occupied elsewhere and didn't notice Dora shirking the end of her shift. The train passengers had all returned to their cars by now. The only customers who lingered were hotel guests. With a quick glance about the room, Dora slid through the door into the hotel lobby.

She wove through the room, her feet barely touching the ground. She couldn't decide if she was angry or happy to see Jake again. She'd expected him never to return, and now that he had . . . What did that mean? She wasn't prepared for this.

In her room, she hurried to put on her winter things. Jake's scrawled note had asked her to meet him by the old footbridge near the creek. It was a good place, far from prying eyes and ears, but cold. At the back door to the hotel, Dora tightened the hood around her head.

Outside it was crisp and sunny. The snow sent prisms of light off in every direction, and Dora blinked the brightness away as she walked to the creek. Once there, it didn't take long to find him. He stood, tall and sure of himself, as usual, by the old bridge that crossed the creek. Dora tried to walk at a stately pace. As excited as she was to see him again, she was still mad. He'd treated her poorly and before she would speak to him about anything, she wanted an apology.

"I wasn't certain you'd come," he said, his hands behind him and his face a bit sheepish.

"Neither was I." It was a stretch of the truth, but he deserved to wriggle a little. She kept a slight distance from him, enough to let him know she could easily turn and leave him here.

"Dora, I need to apologize to you." He moved his hands from behind him to the pockets of his coat. It was if he didn't really know where to put them at all. "I'm sorry. I'm sorry for leaving without any notice, and I'm especially sorry for making you feel as if you'd done something wrong."

"You thought I was the thief," she said. There was no use dancing around it. She'd danced around too many things in her life lately, avoiding conflict at all costs and trying to blend in. And frankly, she was tired of it.

He closed his eyes briefly before opening them again. "I did. I had no other suspects and you were there."

"I've never stolen anything in my life." She clasped her hands in front of her. He had to believe that. Despite all the secrets she'd kept, she was being absolutely honest right now.

"I believe you," he said quietly.

The warmth in his words nearly made her forget the cold around them. He did believe her. Her entire body felt as light as a feather.

"I also believe you're hiding something else from me."

She swallowed and scraped for the courage she needed to speak. "I believe the same of you."

A wry grin curved his lips. "You would be correct, my Dora."

*My Dora*. Her heart picked up pace and she fought to keep her thoughts straight. He might not call her such a thing once he knew who she was. And she may not wish him to once she learned his truth.

Suddenly desperate to stay in the world they'd created for themselves before the truth came crashing into them, Dora blurted out, "I know who the thief is."

The grin disappeared from his face. "I don't think it's your friend, the redheaded one."

"No, it isn't." Dora told him about bringing Mrs. McFarland her tray the night before and what she'd discovered about the money and the safe. "I imagine since she's alone, she feels safe in doing that. But almost each night, she receives one visitor after the dinner service is completed."

Jake furrowed his brow. "Her husband? I don't think he's stealing from the hotel."

"No. Last night, it was me. But every other night, it's another Gilbert Girl. Edie Dutton. She brings Mrs. McFarland coffee and cake." She waited a moment to let the truth sink in. When he nodded, she continued. "You've met her at least once. She was the one who, well . . . She entered the stables when we were . . . there." The memory of how close he'd stood to her that night flooded every sense. She could almost feel his hand on her face and hear the sound of her own heart, all over again.

"Yes, I remember." His gray eyes held her own as he smiled again.

Dora shifted in the snow, not sure if she wished to return to that moment in the barn or if she wanted to run for the safety of her room.

"Wasn't she searching for men who were already at dinner?" he said.

Dora looked at the ground to force her mind to work. "Yes."

"We'd gone about it all wrong," he mused. "I'll tell McFarland. If it is this Miss Dutton, it should be fairly easy to catch her in the act, now that we know when she's taking the money."

Dora smiled, but inside she felt just as bad as she did when she'd suspected Millie. Granted, she hadn't known Edie as long. The girl had only been at the hotel for about a month, but she'd been nothing but nice. She was quiet, like Dora, and Dora supposed she felt a bit of kinship toward the girl for that exact reason. "I wonder why she's been stealing."

"Perhaps she'll tell us once we've put a stop to it," Jake replied.

A silence hung between them. Dora knew what would come next—what was on both their minds.

"I—" he said.

"Could we talk about it later? I must return to the hotel." The words rushed out of her mouth. While she wasn't expected anywhere, it was quite possible someone might go looking for her. And while she wanted the truth so badly for each of them, she also wanted to postpone it. She didn't know why exactly. Maybe it was so they could finish the investigation they'd started without also trying to sort out their feelings for one another. Maybe it was fear. Or maybe she simply wanted to live a bit longer in the possibility that it might work between them.

She took a step backward, and Jake reached for her hand. She let him take it, grateful to have even this one small moment with him.

"Will you be there tonight?" he asked. "You deserve to see this come to a conclusion."

Dora nodded.

"I'll get word to you about where, after I speak with McFarland."

"All right." She stood there a bit longer, not wanting him to let go. She tried to remember every detail of this moment, from the way his large hand nearly covered her smaller one, to the sun that made everything seem just a bit brighter than normal, to the way he watched her as if he could do so forever. Perhaps she imagined that last part, but she didn't care. Not right now. Not when this might be the memory she would relive for the rest of her life, the last perfect moment with a man she feared she loved but couldn't have.

"I'll see you this evening, Dora." He said her name with such warmth she thought he might singlehandedly turn the winter into spring. He squeezed her hand once before letting go.

She dared one glance backward as she walked through the snow toward the break in the tree line. He watched her from the bridge, his hands in his pockets.

And in that moment, Dora knew what she wanted more than anything else in the world. It was selfish and unreasonable and unlikely to happen, but she wanted Jake James holding her hand for the rest of her life.

# Chapter Twenty-eight

The dressing screen was barely large enough for two men to hide behind, but McFarland refused to leave his wife alone with a possible thief, and Jacob needed to lay eyes on the actual stealing to be satisfied. Dora waited in the laundry room nearby. If she was correct, and Miss Dutton was the one stealing from the hotel, Jacob planned to tell McFarland that Dora had been the one to solve the mystery. For now, all McFarland knew was that one of the waitresses had come to Jacob with concern that Miss Dutton might be stealing the money when she delivered dessert to Mrs. McFarland.

There was a knock on the door. Mrs. McFarland glanced their way, nerves tracing every inch of her face. Her husband nodded to her, and that must have been all she needed because she smoothed her skirts, replaced the fearful look on her face with a pleasant one, and went to answer the door. Perhaps one day, if Dora accepted him even after his lies, he might have that sort of unspoken trust with her.

Jake shook his head just slightly. There was plenty of time to think about Dora after this. Right now, he needed to concentrate on the action in front of him.

"Good evening, Mrs. McFarland," a voice with a quiet, nervous timbre floated in from the doorway.

"Edie, my dear," Mrs. McFarland replied. "I do hope you're well. Dora told me you'd been ill."

"I am, thank you." A slight, bespectacled girl emerged into the room, partially hidden by the door and by the dressing screen behind which Jacob had concealed himself. She was as Dora had said, the one who'd discovered them in the stables. The tray shook just slightly in her hands. She looked like the last person in the world who could be stealing hundreds of dollars at a time.

"Mrs. Ruby said they would be serving the spice cake tonight." Mrs. McFarland didn't show any degree of nervousness. Jacob's admiration for the woman grew by the moment.

"Yes. It's quite good, I heard." Miss Dutton set the tray on Mrs. McFarland's desk—the one covered in notes and stacks of bills. When she turned back to face Mrs. McFarland, her eyes stayed just a half-moment longer on the money.

"Let me find you something new to read." Mrs. McFarland bustled past the girl and the desk, turning to survey the shelves on the wall, the ones that were filled with books.

In a split second, Miss Dutton was across the room, just a couple feet away from the dressing screen in front of the open safe. With a quick glance back at Mrs. McFarland, she reached inside, grabbed a stack of bills tied together with string, and dropped them into a pocket in her skirts. She returned to the center of the room before Mrs. McFarland had even spoken again.

McFarland lurched to the side, ready to confront the girl, but Jacob grabbed hold of his sleeve. When the man looked at him, Jacob shook his head. There was something more going on here. He didn't know what, but he felt it in his gut. This wasn't the sort of girl who stole for her own benefit. She was too nervous, even if her movements had become practiced over time.

"I enjoyed the one about birds," the girl said.

"Then how about this one?" Mrs. McFarland turned and presented a red-covered book to Miss Dutton. "It's a study of mountain wildflowers and their uses."

"That sounds wonderful." Miss Dutton hugged the book to her chest. "Thank you." Her hands still shook just slightly, likely to be unnoticed by anyone who didn't suspect her.

"I hope you enjoy it. And thank you for bringing me a tray." Mrs. McFarland glanced toward the screen before showing the girl to the door.

The second she'd left, Jacob strode out from behind the screen. "We'll follow her," he said.

"Do you suppose she isn't working alone?" McFarland asked.

Jacob nodded before slipping the door open. Miss Dutton moved down the hallway, back toward the lobby. Jacob darted quickly to the laundry room door and Dora opened it.

"You were right, and I suspect she's working with someone else," he said quickly. "Will you follow her? She's less likely to think anything of you being nearby. McFarland and I will be just behind you." He didn't like asking her to do this. After all, there was no way to know who she might be going to meet, but this seemed the most likely possibility of finally putting an end to these thefts. "Don't follow her too closely, for your own safety. Please."

Dora nodded her agreement. "I want this finished as much as you do. I'll be careful." She scurried down the hall in the direction Jacob pointed.

"I'll tell you later," Jacob said to a stunned McFarland. For now, he hurried to keep a good pace behind Dora, McFarland by his side.

Miss Dutton wound her way through the emptying lobby, and then down the south wing hallway to the kitchen door. Dora slipped in behind her, while Jacob and McFarland hung back so as not to arouse suspicion. Jacob peered in through the door a moment later, only to see Dora's form exiting the outside door. He gestured to McFarland, and they followed.

They paused again before leaving the hotel through the kitchen door. Outside, the air bit through Jacob's shirtsleeves. They hadn't a spare moment to grab coats or any other protective clothing. Jacob only hoped they wouldn't be out here long, else they'd all freeze to death instead of catching the thieves.

Ahead, he could just barely make out Dora following Miss Dutton in the direction of the stables. The wind picked up as Miss Dutton entered the building. Jacob drew his chin down, attempting to fight the chill air that whispered down his collar. Next to him, McFarland did the same, with some more colorful language to accompany the action.

Dora paused by the stable door, and at that very moment, Jacob saw the flaw in his plan.

"Remain outside!" he shouted, but his words were lost in the wind.

Dora reached to push open the door, and Jacob broke into a run. The frozen air bit at the insides of his nose and mouth, but he didn't care. All that mattered was preventing Dora from walking into what might be a terribly dangerous situation. "Dora!"

Again, she didn't hear him. Instead, she disappeared inside.

# Chapter Twenty-nine

D ora could barely breathe. When she'd peeked in through the stable door, she hadn't seen a soul and thought that perhaps they'd gone to the rear of the building. But now, firmly inside with the door shut behind her, she found she was wrong.

With the dim light from the few lamps that hung from pegs and sat on the little table, it had been impossible to see Edie standing inside, in conversation with one of the stablehands. A Mr. Adkins, if Dora remembered correctly. He hadn't been at the hotel for very long.

"Dora!" Edie shoved something into the folds of the cloak she'd pulled from the peg near the kitchen door. "Why are you here so late?"

"I . . ." Her mind searched for an explanation. It was hard to think with her heart pounding so loudly and her frozen hands trembling. She couldn't come out and accuse Edie of stealing, not with Mr. Adkins right here and not when she wasn't certain if he was involved. "I saw you leave and was worried."

"Oh. I'm fine. You needn't worry," Edie said, although the slight tremble in her voice said otherwise.

"Miss Dutton has taken a liking to the horses," Mr. Adkins said.

It was awfully late to visit horses, particularly when doing so alone with a stablehand was strictly against hotel rules. Although there wasn't much Dora could say about that, considering how frequently she'd broken that rule. At a loss for how to reply, Dora moved away from the door and ran her hands up and down her arms to warm herself.

"I'm glad you're here," Edie said. "Perhaps you'll accompany me back to the hotel once I've had my visit?"

Just as Dora was about to speak, the stable door opened. A gust of wind blew in with Jake and Mr. McFarland. Dora had never been so grateful to see two people in her life.

"Miss Dutton, Mr. Adkins," McFarland said as if he was here for polite conversation. Jake glanced at both of them but didn't bother to issue a greeting.

"Are you in need of horses?" Mr. Adkins asked.

Edie inched closer to Dora. Her features were shadowed, but her hands were empty. She no longer had what Dora assumed to be the money she'd stolen from the safe. She must have given it to Mr. Adkins while Dora was busy trying to warm herself.

"We are not," Jake said, his words clipped.

Mr. Adkins cast a quick glance at Edie, frowning. She shook her head. "I don't suppose you gentlemen will excuse me, then. It's high time I took my rest. Morning comes early for me and Robbins." He moved in front of Edie and Dora as he spoke.

Something about the situation made the little hairs on Dora's arms rise. There was no door, besides the one that led outside, at this end of the stables and no ladder or stairs that led upstairs. That meant the stablehands bunked elsewhere, likely at the far end. Perhaps he wanted to douse the lamps before turning in. But his tense figure, standing now between her and the other men, made her think otherwise.

"I don't suppose you'll turn out your pockets for us, Adkins?" Jake said.

Beside Dora, Edie drew in a gasp of breath. Dora felt the girl look at her, but she kept her own eyes fixed on the situation in front of her, unable to shake the uneasy feeling that she'd rather be closer to Jake and McFarland than trapped in this corner with no way out.

"I'm sorry?" Mr. Adkins said.

"You heard me," Jake replied.

"Mr. McFarland, I must—" Mr. Adkins began.

"Do as the man asks." Mr. McFarland's Irish brogue sounded even more pronounced. He turned to Jake. "It may still be with the girl."

"It isn't." Dora piped up, forcing the words out around the nerves that threatened to start her entire body trembling.

Mr. Adkins turned quickly and assessed her before returning his attention to the men. "Gentlemen, I don't know what this is about, but might we postpone this conversation until morning? I must be up early with the horses."

Jake laughed, but the sound was hollow and impatient. "Considering we just saw Miss Dutton steal a stack of money from the hotel office and then come directly here, no—this can't wait until morning."

The stables were silent save for the sounds of the horses and the echo of Jake's words hanging in the air. And then everything happened at once. Jake took a step forward. Mr. Adkins drew a revolver. Edie shrieked when he grabbed her arm and pulled her in front of him.

"Dora!" Jake yelled, a second too late.

His voice awoke something inside her—a voice that screamed, *Run*! But the very moment she began to move, Mr. Adkins' hand clamped around her wrist and dragged her in front of him too. She pulled against his grip, but all that did was make him hold on even tighter. Edie stood perfectly still, with Mr. Adkins' arm wrapped around her neck. Fighting him was getting Dora nowhere except out of breath. She stopped, her heart beating so fast she thought she might be sick.

Jake's face was anguished, his hands clenched into fists at his sides as Mr. McFarland's hand gripped his shoulder. "What do you want?" The words sounded as if he'd ground them out between his teeth.

"To leave, that's all. A couple of saddled horses should get us out of here nicely," Mr. Adkins said, not loosening his grip even a little.

"Us?" Jake said at the same time Mr. McFarland added, "You aren't taking these girls anywhere."

Mr. Adkins laughed. "I believe you're in no position to tell me what I can or cannot do, gentlemen. Now, two horses, please. The ladies can share one."

The very thought of going anywhere with this man made Dora pull against his grip again. This time he responded by yanking her right up in front of him, next to Edie, and letting go of her wrist only to wrap his arm around her waist. She struggled against him, desperate to be anywhere that wasn't so close to this awful man, but he'd pinned her arms against her sides. Across from them, Jake's eyes seemed to blaze fire in the shadowy light.

"Now," Mr. Adkins said.

"I want to know why, first," Jake said, still as tense as a piece of iron.

"Why do you care so much?" Mr. Adkins asked.

Dora held her breath. Would he confess he was a detective? Another thought then occurred to her, one that could've knocked her sideways if she wasn't already pinched against the awful Mr. Adkins—if Jake was a detective, where was his gun? What sort of detective went about unarmed, particularly when he knew he might be facing his quarry?

The look on Jake's face confirmed her confusion. Instead of deflecting Mr. Adkins' question or announcing himself as a detective, his features went as hard as rock.

He was angry.

Mr. McFarland must have seen it too, because he grabbed Jake's other shoulder with his free hand to keep him in place.

"This hotel supports every single person who works for it. Your thievery has ensured that paying each employee at the end of this month will be difficult, if not impossible." Jake spat the words at Mr. Adkins.

Dora wanted so badly to go to him. No matter his secrets, he truly cared for all the employees of the hotel. He'd worked hard to find the thief so they could all keep their positions here and the hotel could remain open. That alone meant everything to her.

"The company that owns this place is richer than any of us can imagine," Mr. Adkins replied. "It's no skin off their backs to send as much money as is needed to keep the hotel open. Anything Miss Edie here pilfered is just pennies to them."

"That's my family," Jake said, so low Dora thought she might not have heard him correctly.

Mr. Adkins said nothing at first. And then he laughed, short but clearly disbelieving.

"It's not a joke," Jake said harshly. "My name is Jacob Gilbert, and that, Mr. Adkins, is my family you've stolen from." He shrugged off Mr. McFarland's grip as he stepped forward.

Dora blinked at him, all the memories rushing back at her, piecing themselves together in a way that finally made sense. His telegram, his well-to-do friends, his assumption that many opportunities were available for the poor. He was wealthy. More than that, he *owned* the hotel where Dora worked. The world seemed to go dizzy, and she gripped Mr. Adkins' arm as she shut her eyes.

If she survived this night, telling him her own secret was the last thing she would do now.

# Chapter Thirty

The blood rushed in Jacob's ears. McFarland's hands had gone slack on his shoulders, but Jacob's attention was on Dora. This wasn't how he wanted her to find out. He'd imagined telling her when they were alone, and asking her forgiveness for not being honest with her from the beginning. But now . . . in the dimness of the stables, he could barely see her eyes, but her body seemed to go slack. He wanted to go to her, take her in his arms, and whisper how sorry he was into her hair.

"Well, isn't that interesting," Adkins drawled. If he was surprised, he'd gotten over it quickly. He jerked his head toward the stalls that lined the stables to Jacob's left. "Now how about you saddle me up two horses, Mr. Gilbert? Hurry now, before McFarland here confesses to being the king of England." The man chuckled at his own joke.

Jacob's hands tightened into fists again. He wanted, more than anything, to land one of them squarely into Adkins' jaw. But he couldn't, not while Adkins had the girls held at gunpoint. He couldn't take the chance.

"Go," McFarland whispered.

Jacob turned and stared at him. The man nodded. For the life of him, Jacob couldn't figure out what the man had planned—until Jacob grabbed the lamp hanging from the nail nearby and taken a few steps toward the rear of the stables. There, hunched beside an open, empty stall door, was Robbins. The older round man held a shovel.

Jacob locked eyes with him but said nothing. He stopped a couple of stalls down and fumbled with hanging the lamp, his eyes on Adkins, the girls, and McFarland.

McFarland stepped farther into the stables. "Forgive me, Mr. Adkins. It's a mite cold in here and these old bones need to get away from that door."

Adkins turned, forcing the girls around with him as he kept his eyes on Mc-
Farland. His back was completely against the posts that held up the first horse
stall. He seemed to figure out a second too late that McFarland had forced him
to turn his back on Jacob. McFarland likely figured Jacob would attempt something from behind Adkins, and he was right—except it wouldn't be Jacob.

"Get back over there." Adkins waved his revolver toward where McFarland
had been standing near the door.

"Just a moment now—let me get warmed up."

"Now," Adkins growled out. He twisted back to find Jacob in the darkness.
Seemingly satisfied that Jacob was busy with the horses, he returned his attention to McFarland.

"All right, all right." McFarland took one step toward the door, and that was
when Frank Robbins sprang up.

Quicker than Jacob would've ever given him credit for, Robbins brought
the back of the shovel down onto Adkins' head. The man stumbled forward,
loosening his hold on the girls enough for them both to run toward McFarland.
He still held the gun, however, even as he clasped his free hand to his head.
"What . . .?" He turned, and Jacob was there.

He threw himself into Adkins and sent the revolver flying to the floor. Out
of the corner of his eye, he spotted McFarland grabbing it from where it landed. Adkins was breathing hard but still fighting. Jacob landed one good punch
to the man's jaw. The pain from the impact radiated up his arm. He hadn't been
in a fight since his university days in New York, and even then, it was more for
sport than anything else. The tingling in his arm disappeared the moment Adkins brought a knee into Jacob's stomach.

Gasping for air, he fell to the side. It was over. He didn't want to see Dora's
face. Her disappointment in him would be worse than being bested by this sorry excuse for a man.

"James!"

Why was someone calling for his brother? Jacob turned his head slightly to
the side. McFarland was there, holding Adkins down.

"Gilbert!" he said this time.

The fog cleared. Jacob drew in a rattling breath and forced himself to his
hands and knees. Maybe this wasn't over after all. McFarland wouldn't be able
to hold the man down long.

"Jake, here." Dora stood over him, a length of rope in her hands. She gazed at him, fierce pride in her eyes. He had to move, for her. He took the rope from her, and breathing began to come a bit easier.

Together, he and McFarland bound Adkins and propped him against one of the wooden posts. Jacob leaned against a post himself, feeling more bruised and battered than he had in years. Dora flew to his side, her hands on his face and arms until she seemed satisfied he wasn't permanently injured. He placed a hand on either side of her face. She was here, she was whole, and despite that coward Adkins' best efforts, she was unharmed. If he'd hurt her in any way, Jacob was certain of one thing—the man wouldn't be alive right now.

McFarland stood by silently until Jacob remembered they had an audience that not only included McFarland, but Adkins, Miss Dutton, and Frank Robbins, who stood nearby. He slowly withdrew his hands, letting them hang uselessly at his sides.

McFarland cleared his throat. "I'd enjoy a thorough accounting of how Miss Reynolds became involved in this affair later. Her well-being is still my charge, no matter your association with the Gilbert Company."

Jacob placed a hand on his stomach, drawing a still-painful breath. "I promise you I've taken no liberties with Miss Reynolds." He was being broad with his definition of "liberties," but McFarland didn't need to know that.

McFarland nodded, although his face belied his true feelings on the subject, and they weren't happy ones. "I sent for the sheriff up in Cañon City earlier tonight. I imagine he'll arrive in the morning."

Jacob nodded toward Miss Dutton, who stood like a mouse against the stable wall, her face wet with tears. "And what of Miss Dutton?"

"Shouldn't we hear what she has to say before deciding her fate?" Dora said. She remained by Jacob's side, and all he wanted to do was make everyone else disappear from the stables so he could take her into his arms. He had so much to say to her.

Dora moved away from him to stand near Miss Dutton. "Edie?" she prodded.

The girl looked up at them all, her face shining in the light from the lantern hanging nearby. She removed her glasses and wiped her face with her hand. "I'm so sorry," she finally said in a garbled voice. "I . . . I know it doesn't excuse my actions, but I was given no choice."

"What do you mean?" Dora asked. She stood with her arms crossed, but her head tilted in sympathy.

"Pay no attention to her lies," Adkins said from his seat on the floor. He spat into the straw.

Robbins nudged him with the toe of his boot. "Let the lady speak."

Miss Dutton pulled at her gloves. "He followed me here from Kansas. My family . . .well, we owed him money. He came to collect."

"By forcing you to steal from the hotel," McFarland finished for her. The disgust in his face echoed Jacob's exact feelings.

"Is that true?" Jacob asked Adkins.

"Weren't no other way she could've paid me what she owed quick enough," he said.

Jacob caught McFarland's eye. He shook his head, indicating he didn't wish to press any charges against Miss Dutton. Clearly, the poor girl was sorrowful over what she'd done, and hadn't wanted to take the money to begin with. While that determination was ultimately up to Jacob, it remained McFarland's decision whether the girl would stay or go.

"Mr. McFarland," Dora said softly. "If I may, I believe you should give Edie another chance here. She's a hard worker, and without the specter of Mr. Adkins forcing her to make terrible choices, I'm certain she'll be an asset to the dining room."

Jacob's heart swelled with pride. It was Miss Dutton's fault that Dora had been in this situation, that she could've been hurt by Mr. Adkins. And yet, here she was, vouching to give the girl a second chance.

McFarland clasped his hands behind him. "That is quite a convincing testimony, Miss Reynolds. Miss Dutton, do you wish to remain in your position here?"

The girl wiped more tears from her face. "Oh, yes! I apologize for what has happened, and I promise to be the model waitress from now on. If you decide to let me stay, that is." She ducked her head.

"You can stay, under two conditions," McFarland replied. "One, you do nothing—absolutely nothing—that could besmirch the name of this hotel or put it into jeopardy. And two, if you ever find yourself in such a predicament again, you come to me instead of simply caving to the demands of a coward like Mr. Adkins."

Miss Dutton smiled timidly. "Yes, of course. I promise."

"One more thing," McFarland said. "Do not speak of this to anyone else. For the sake of my own reputation, I can't have any of my employees thinking I've gone soft. Or the Gilbert family, for that matter." He glanced at Jake.

Jacob tried not to laugh. "Your secret is safe with me."

"That goes for you too." McFarland pointed at Robbins and Dora. "Robbins, help me get this sorry excuse for a man up to the hotel. Miss Dutton, will you lead the way?" They hoisted hands under Adkins' arms and hauled him to his feet. Just before leaving the stables, McFarland glanced back at Jacob. "I expect a thorough explanation tomorrow."

When Jacob nodded his assent, McFarland shook his head. "I'm going soft, that's all there is to it."

Dora covered her smile with a hand as they left. The second the door shut, Jacob turned his grin to her. He reached for her hand. She let him take it, but when she finally turned to meet his eyes, she wasn't smiling.

Foreboding thumped through his body. "Dora?" he finally dared to ask.

She gently pulled her hand from his grip. "I can't," she said.

# Chapter Thirty-one

Jake's eyebrows drew together. "That wasn't the way in which I'd intended for you to find out. I wasn't honest with you, and I apologize for that. I wanted to tell you so many times, but I was bound by promises to my family to find the thief. I know that doesn't make lying to you right, but I hope you understand."

Dora twisted a fold of her skirt between her fingers. The revelation had been jarring, of course, but it made telling him who she really was even harder. "I hadn't expected you to be a Gilbert, of course, but I'd had the feeling you weren't who you'd presented yourself to be."

"Was I that bad at being Jake James?" He gave her a crooked grin, and she would've given him the world if she could.

"Not at all. In fact, I quite liked Jake James." The words were out of her mouth before she even realized what she was saying. Thankfully, the darkness inside the stables might make it more difficult for Jake—or Jacob, she supposed—to see the flush that had crept up into her cheeks.

"I do too. I suppose I'm stuck with remaining a Gilbert, but I wouldn't be opposed to being Jake from here on out." He frowned just slightly, enough to alert Dora that there was something else he hadn't told her.

"Jake?" Dora tentatively placed a hand on his arm before realizing she shouldn't. She still hadn't told him about herself. And now that she was here, and the moment was right, she didn't know if she could. Not after finding out who he was.

He swallowed visibly and caught her hand as she pulled it away. "Dora. I had a long while to think on the train to and from Denver. I was wrong to suspect you of stealing the money, and I want you to know that I'm truly sorry. But I came to understand that I had a good reason for that suspicion. And that's because you haven't been entirely honest with me about yourself."

She closed her eyes and nodded, reveling in the sensation of her hand in his. It might be for the last time, and she wanted to be able to recall the memory after she'd returned home, alone.

"Tell me. Please." His voice was low and achingly sweet.

Dora forced herself to open her eyes and look at him. Every inch of him was focused on her. "I'm afraid you'll no longer care for me once you know." It hurt to say the words out loud, but she was no fool. Few white men felt any affection at all toward her people. It had been as if they were simply in the way, to be shoved aside in the name of progress, expected to accept their fates and stay put.

Dora hadn't.

She drew in a deep breath. She had nothing to be ashamed of. She was proud of her family, of her tribe. Whether Jake accepted that was his decision. "I'm not from Chicago."

His face was impassive. "I'd figured as much." He gave her hand a squeeze, encouragement to continue. And she wondered if he'd feel the same way in a few minutes' time.

"I'm from the Territory, just a few days' ride southwest of here, now. But originally, my people are of this valley, these mountains, and all the land surrounding it."

He tilted his head, clearly confused.

She pulled her hand from his again. If she was going to do this, she would do it on her own—with her own courage, her own breath, and her own identity. She rested her hands at her sides before she continued. "My mother is Ute. I don't know my father. He left when I was young, after marrying my mother and having second thoughts. But I've been told he was a soldier from Maryland."

She paused a moment, giving Jake time to react. She didn't know what she expected him to do, but it wasn't simply remaining still and then asking her. "You've never met your father?"

Stunned that the fact he decided to question was that one, she said, "No, not that I can remember. His name was Reynolds. My mother shed the name after he left, but I adopted it when I came here."

"And you've kept this to yourself all this time?"

She nodded. "I disliked lying about who I am, but I needed the work so badly. My mother . . . my family . . ." She stopped a second to choke back the tears that clogged her throat. "They aren't faring well on the reservation. It's as if all the life has gone out of my uncles, and my cousins have no hope for what the future might bring. Sickness is rampant, and food is scarce. With money, they can purchase more than what is offered. But of course, there is no way to earn money there. Someone had to leave, even though that's disallowed too. I speak perfect English, so my mother and I decided I would be the one to go. The rest of the family knows I'm working, but they don't know where."

His jaw worked as he studied her. He didn't smile, but he didn't look angry either. "How did you come to find work here?"

"I made my way to Denver, where I saw an advertisement for Gilbert Girls in the newspaper. I presented myself as Dora Reynolds from Chicago, of a good, hardworking family, and was awarded the job." She paused, looking him in the eye. "Because, as I'm sure you know, the Gilbert Company only advertises for white girls."

He closed his eyes for a brief moment before opening them again. "I'm aware. And I'm . . ." He shook his head but didn't finish.

"Now that you know my secret, I must beseech you to keep it and let me remain here. My family depends on me. I don't know what will happen if I don't . ." Tears choked her throat, threatening to break through the brave facade she wore.

"Dora," Jake said softly. "I'm not going to give you away."

It felt as if the walls of her heart had collapsed. She could continue to work. Her family would be safe. "I don't know how I can ever thank you—"

Before she had time to think through what was happening, he'd closed the gap between them. Placing a hand lightly on her cheek, he lowered his face until his mouth was a fraction of an inch from hers.

Dora drew in a sharp breath. Thoughts tumbled through her head, none of them clear enough to make sense save for one—he didn't care that she wasn't Dora Reynolds of Chicago. "Jake?" she whispered, but her voice was lost as he dropped his lips to hers.

All of the fear and uncertainty and secrets she'd kept to herself for months disappeared in that one kiss. She lifted her hands to his shoulders as both of his hands held her face. Nothing could ever harm her here, not when she was with him. He wouldn't let it happen, and she knew that as sure as she knew the love of her own family.

He drew away, a warm smile crossing his face. "Dora Reynolds, I love you."

She blinked at him, knowing she felt the same way. She never wanted another moment without his hand covering hers or that smile warming her very bones. "I . . . I didn't think . . ."

"Then don't," he said, his thumb tracing an arc on her cheekbone.

A happy warmth curled through Dora's body despite the cold that lurked in the air. "I love you, too."

Jake grinned and dropped his hands to grip hers. "Are you certain?"

She laughed. What sort of question was that? "With all my heart."

"Then I have a question I must pose to you, but first you should know that my meeting in Denver—with my father—did not go well." He looked down at her hands, the smile gone from his face. "He'll be happy we've found the thief, but I didn't leave his office on good terms. Essentially . . ." He finally drew his head back up to meet her eyes. "I'm on my own. I have nothing, Dora, save for my education and my charm." He smiled a little at his own words, but the expression disappeared quickly.

"You have more than that," she said, gripping his hands tightly. "You're intelligent and quick-witted. A hard worker. You're kind and generous with your time. Even without money, you have far more opportunities than any man in my family simply by virtue of your birth."

He frowned and she feared she might have said too much with her last words. But it was the truth, and Jake should know how lucky he was. He might not ever know the closeness and love of growing up in a family like hers, but the world was his for the taking.

"What do you want to do?" Dora asked.

"I don't know. Not yet. For now, I suppose I'm happy working at the hotel if McFarland will have me back."

Dora smiled at him. He would figure it out, with time. Jake was not one to sit still for long. "Then that's what you should do."

"I . . ." He cleared his throat and looked down at her hands again before meeting her eyes. "I wanted to ask you if you'd consider marrying me. I haven't anything to offer you beyond myself. I don't even know if I still have a position here. But I'll work hard, and perhaps I can build something great, with you at my side."

The last wall within Dora crumbled with barely a protest. He wished to marry her. It was more than she'd ever dared to dream, not since deciding to leave the reservation to find work. Work . . . how would she support her family if she married?

As if reading her thoughts, Jake said, "I know you worry about your family. I promise we'll continue to send them any funds we can. If McFarland will have me back, I'll explain the situation to him—carefully," he added upon seeing the fear that crossed her face. "I'm certain he'll agree to pay me a little more. I promise you that your family won't suffer. After all, they'll be my family too."

His words were all she needed. "Then yes. I'll marry you, Jake Gilbert." Dora couldn't keep the smile from her face, and he returned it.

Jake drew her to him. "I promise I'll do everything I can to make you happy, my Dora."

"You already do." She tilted her head back to see his face. And she knew she'd never be happier in her life. He was her home, her heart, and her everything.

Forever.

# Epilogue

"I don't need a special dress," Dora said over a heap of skirts and bodices in her arms.

"Oh, hush. You're getting married. You deserve something beautiful to wear." Penny retrieved a skirt the color of spring grasses from Caroline's wardrobe.

"I wish you had more time," Caroline said as she took the pile of clothing from Dora's arms. "I would've made you something, like I am for Penny."

"It's all right." Dora stretched her aching arms. Who knew clothing could weigh so much? Then again, Dora hadn't known anyone could own so many dresses until she'd met Caroline. "All I want is to marry Jake, and a wedding with Penny and Sheriff Young is perfect." She'd told Penny and Caroline about her family and where she'd come from not long after she'd told Jake. Each of them had reacted differently, as she'd expected, but they'd both accepted her with love. They'd promised to keep her secret to themselves, agreeing that everyone might not feel the same way. Dora had never been so grateful for friends such as these. In a way, leaving her family had been the best choice she'd ever made, as much as she missed them each day.

"This one!" Penny held out a deep blue set of skirts and matching bodice. "This would look lovely on you." She placed the bodice under Dora's chin. "Caroline?"

Caroline nodded. "It's almost as if that color was made for you. Mr. Gilbert won't be able to look away when he sees you in that dress."

Penny handed Dora a small mirror. Her friends were right. The color made her skin glow and her hair look even more vivid. She placed the mirror on Caroline's dressing table. "Would it be all right if I wore this dress?"

"Of course." Caroline's smile was almost brighter than the snow sparkling in the sun outside the window. "Try it on, and we'll see if it needs any tailoring."

"Just think," Penny said as she replaced skirts and bodices back in Caroline's wardrobe. "Only two more weeks and we'll be married! And you'll be marrying an owner of the hotel!"

"He's not. He's just a desk clerk," Dora corrected her friend. Although she didn't expect Jake to remain in that position for long. He was already mentioning various ideas for businesses he thought their little place in the valley needed.

"Oh, pish. He's a Gilbert!" Penny held a gold and yellow bodice to herself and admired it. "It shouldn't be long before Emma's arrived either."

Dora smiled at the thought of seeing her friend again for the first time in months. "They must be on their way now."

"And it will be Christmas!" Caroline added. "I have so many ideas for decorating the store."

"Let us know if you need help," Dora said. Although she hadn't grown up celebrating Christmas, she was looking forward to the holiday. All the girls were talking of their traditions at home, and Mrs. McFarland and Mrs. Ruby were beginning to plan special Christmas menus and decorations for the hotel. And now that she was getting married on Christmas, Dora decided it might be her new favorite day of the year.

"Oh!" Penny clasped her hands together, her eyes shining. "I almost forgot! Have you told Caroline of your idea?"

Color began to flood Dora's cheeks. She'd been so nervous to share her thoughts with Penny, but both she and Millie had thought the idea to be wonderful. She hoped Caroline might think the same. After all, she may need her friends' help if it turned out to be successful.

"Go on," Penny said impatiently. "Tell her."

Dora ran a finger over the pleats in the skirt of the blue dress. "On his way to Denver, Jake met a man who was traveling to fetch his intended—whom he'd never met."

Caroline raised her eyebrows, while Penny nearly squealed with excitement.

"He'd written off to a service back East for a mail-order bride. They'd placed his request in a newspaper, a woman answered it, they exchanged a few letters, and now they're to be married."

"I've heard of such things," Caroline said.

"Isn't it the most romantic?" Penny hugged her arms to herself.

"It's terrifying. What if the man turns out to be a drunk or an outlaw or . . . or worse?" Caroline shuddered. She'd once been engaged to a terrible man, and Dora knew he was exactly the sort she had in mind for her worries.

"What if the service met the men first, to ensure they're worthy of marriage?" Dora asked.

Caroline nodded slowly. "That might work. It would lend an air of respectability to the whole thing, too."

Dora drew in a deep breath. "I'd like to start such a service here, in Crest Stone, with Jake's help. And yours, too, if you're able. Penny's agreed to help, as best she can from Cañon City."

A slow smile crossed Caroline's face. "It would be fun. And I imagine the service would be useful, if what Thomas and everyone thinks will happen next year comes true." Their little stop on the railroad was poised to become a full-fledged town, with Emma's husband returning to oversee some of the building.

"You'll join us?" Penny asked.

"Yes, so long as it doesn't interfere with my duties here at the store and so long as Thomas doesn't mind it."

Dora clasped her arms around her friend. "Thank you, for everything. My dress and helping with this new venture." She stepped back, smiling more than she'd ever thought possible. "Thank you to both of you."

Penny took both their hands in hers. "Who would have thought this is where we'd be a year ago?"

Both Caroline and Dora shook their heads. Their lives were only just beginning, and Dora couldn't wait to see what happened next.

THANK YOU FOR READING! Now that you've met Dora and Jake, you'll have to find out what happens at their double wedding with Penny and Ben in the next book. I'll give you a hint—it's a Christmas story featuring a heroine mentioned in the first Gilbert Girls book and a wayward cowboy who finds himself stuck at the hotel. That book, *Forever Christmas*, is next. It's available now at http://bit.ly/ForeverChristmasBook. To be alerted about new books—and to find out more about the new Crest Stone mail order brides series—sign up here: http://bit.ly/catsnewsletter I also give subscribers a free

*Gilbert Girls* prequel novella (it tells the story of Mr. and Mrs. McFarland), sneak peeks at upcoming books, insights into the writer life, discounts and deals, inspirations, and so much more. I'd love to have *you* join the fun! You can also find me on Facebook at: http://bit.ly/CatonFacebook and on my website http://bit.ly/CatCahillAuthor

Turn the page to see a complete list of the books in the *Gilbert Girls* series.

# Books in The Gilbert Girls series

Building Forever[1]
Running From Forever[2]
Wild Forever[3]
Hidden Forever[4]
Forever Christmas[5]

---

1. http://bit.ly/BuildingForeverbook

2. http://bit.ly/RunningForeverBook

3. http://bit.ly/WildForeverBook

4. http://bit.ly/HiddenForeverBook

5. http://bit.ly/ForeverChristmasBook

# About the Author, Cat Cahill

A sunset. Snow on the mountains. A roaring river in the spring. A man and a woman who can't fight the love that pulls them together. The danger and uncertainty of life in the Old West. This is what inspires me to write. I hope you find an escape in my books!

I live with my family, my hound dog, and a few cats in Kentucky. When I'm not writing, I'm losing myself in a good book, planning my next travel adventure, doing a puzzle, attempting to garden, or wrangling my kids.

Made in United States
North Haven, CT
24 July 2023

39456710R00086